The Dark Angel was in a tight spot.

She's been paid to break into an oilman's apartment and now his key was turning in the lock!

There was only one move to make. With her mini-shift unzipped to the waist, she swayed voluptuously into the living room.

The man stared, incredulous, at the sexy brown apparition coming towards him. Letting the dress slip from her shoulder, Angie stepped forth, naked except for her frilly pink garter belt, nylon hose, and black high-heeled boots!

"What are *you* planning to do?" he cried out.

And then Angie showed him.

THE EMERALD OIL CAPER

James D. Lawrence

PYRAMID BOOKS NEW YORK

THE EMERALD OIL CAPER

A PYRAMID BOOK

Produced by Lyle Kenyon Engel

Copyright © 1975 by Lyle Kenyon Engel

Pyramid edition published March 1975

ISBN 0-515-03629-3
Library of Congress Catalog Card Number: 74-29105

Printed in the United States of America

Pyramid Books are published by Pyramid Communications, Inc. Its trademarks, consisting of the word "Pyramid" and the portrayal of a pyramid, are registered in the United States Patent Office.

Pyramid Communications, Inc., 919 Third Avenue, New York, N.Y. 10022

CONDITIONS OF SALE

THE EMERALD OIL CAPER

Chapter One

The invitation came scented with danger. Maybe that's why she couldn't resist a nibble. Especially when the bait was long and green.

Angela Harpe, better known to the cops and the underworld as the Dark Angel, was settled for the evening in her plush Manhattan pad in the Turtle Bay Towers, overlooking the East River and the United Nations, when the house phone rang.

"This is Luke, down in the lobby, Miss Harpe," said the reception desk watchman. "Got a letter for you."

At this hour? Angie frowned. "Special delivery?"

"Nope, just a plain white envelope with your name on it. Some chick brought it in. I'd be glad to run it up 'cept I can't leave the desk."

Luke's plaintive tone made it clear that he wasn't kidding. He'd have been only too happy to dash up to the stone fox's apartment. He knew it would have netted him at least a two-buck tip and, more importantly, a throbbing hard-on.

Angela Harpe was brown and beautiful and stacked like the proverbial brick shithouse. And often not overdressed. Once when he knocked, she had come to the door straight out of the shower with her white terry robe flapping open, affording him a breath-stopping peek at her curly black bush.

"If you're, uh, not completely dressed, you could just come down in the elevator," Luke added hopefully, "and I could bring it over to you, so you wouldn't have to step out in the lobby."

Angie gave a deep-throated chuckle, reading his mind. "That's real kind of you, Luke. I'll manage somehow. Thanks."

In point of fact, she was at that moment cozily curled up, stark naked, in her Charles Eames chair, re-reading for the umpteenth time Huxley's *After the Fireworks,* while her hi-fi gave off a muted background tinkle of Wanda Landowska playing a Bach fugue on the harpsichord. In close reach sat a still-steaming cup of coffee spiked with Beefeater gin.

All in all, it was one of those blissfully comfy moments when Angie wouldn't normally have chosen to move what she often termed her black butt. But the letter piqued her curiosity. Besides, more than a week had gone by since she closed her last case, with no fresh excitement looming on the horizon. The Dark Angel was getting a trifle hungry for action.

She pulled a hooded djellaba of peach silk over her ripely swelling nudity and went down in the elevator.

"Wow!" Luke murmured respectfully, handing her the letter. Angie smiled and graciously revolved her hips for him as she ankled back across the marble lobby to the lift.

Her name, *Ms. Angela Harpe,* was written in green ink in a feminine hand on the envelope. Now, back in her apartment, Angie slit it open. Inside was a folded missive. As she went to read it, a one thousand dollar bill dropped out.

Angie did a slight double-take and picked up the bill. Yep, a genuine green big one, with the walrus-mustached face of Grover Cleveland staring back at her dyspeptically.

The letter sounded cryptic but promising:

There's more where this came from.

No signature. Angie reached for the house phone again and buzzed the lobby. "Luke, tell me about the girl who brought this letter."

"What's to tell? She was just another chick."

"How old?"

"Mm, middle twenties, I guess. Straight dark hair. Good-looking. Real nice tush, if you'll pardon the language."

"And you've never seen her before?"

"No, ma'am. Her face didn't mean nothing to me. And I seldom forget a face."

"Or a tush either, I presume. Did you happen to see what she was driving?"

"Didn't notice offhand, Miss Harpe. In fact—stop to think of it, I don't believe she came in a car. I got the impression she just walked in off the street."

A light was flashing insistently on the outside line button of Angie's phone. "Okay, thanks, Luke," she said hastily and pressed the button to switch over. "Hello?"

"Miss Harpe?"

"Speaking."

"By now you must have received my message . . . with the retainer . . . ?" The voice was feminine and slightly husky, with that phonily upper-crust tendency to mush the "s" sounds that always grated peculiarly on Angie's own ghetto-bred, Radcliffe-trained sensibilities.

"I got six words and a G-note, if that's what you're referring to," said Angie. "But I'm afraid I never retain without knowing who's doing the retaining."

"The thousand dollars is yours to keep, whatever

9

happens," said the caller with a sweet and lofty air of benevolence.

"You're so right, baby."

"But we hope you'll want to learn—and earn—more."

"Who's we?"

"Editorial we, so to speak. I'm phoning you now on behalf of my principal."

"And who's he—or she, as the case may be?" Angie inquired.

"That," said the unknown caller, "is the reason for this roundabout way of doing business. You see, it's rather important that he not be seen contacting you—and you not be seen contacting him."

"What's to keep *you* from coming up to my pad?"

"Well, for one thing I'm known as his employee." She hesitated a moment, then swept on, "But I'll explain all that when we meet."

"And when will that fateful event take place?"

"Tonight. At once, if you're agreeable."

"Where?"

"On the street. I'm calling from a sidewalk phone booth near your apartment building. If you'll start walking west, toward Fifth Avenue, we'll meet very shortly."

"Well, from here it wouldn't be too easy to walk *east* toward Fifth Avenue," observed Angie, "short of circumnavigating the globe and walking on water like Our Savior. But aside from that, how'll I know you?"

Again the caller hesitated, this time for the merest fraction of a second. "Well, I'm blonde and I'm wearing a blue dress. But the important thing is that I'll know *you*—so don't worry."

"How nice. I feel completely reassured," said Angie, and hung up.

She sat thoughtfully considering for a moment—but

not very long. As a private eye specializing in the recovery of loot for insurance companies, she had foiled criminal capers totaling hundreds of thousands of dollars in scores—in fact, millions. On one recent case alone, filed under the code name of *The Dream Girl Caper*, she had thwarted a Mafia hijacking of $3,000,000 in contest prize money. So at any given time, there might well be a half dozen contracts out on her life. And what sweeter setup than to call her out of her apartment at night to walk down a dark street in Manhattan, that happy hunting ground of muggers?

On the other hand, she was vulnerable every day of her life. And at this particular moment, spoiling for action.

Angie reached for the phone and called the desk again. "Sorry to keep bothering you, Luke, but about that chick who brought the letter—if you noticed her tush, maybe you can remember what she was wearing. Like a dress, or jeans—or what?"

"Do I remember!" Luke chuckled. "You know it, Miss Harpe! She was wearing some kinda red pantsuit. Fit like it was painted on."

Angela Harpe dressed quickly, lingering for a moment over black velvet jeans before choosing a slinky champagne-colored, front-zipped mini-shift of double-knit polyester. She liked the feeling it gave her of freedom of movement—besides which, like all her minis, its ultra-brevity provided a useful distraction for male eyes in case of any go-for-broke action.

To hype the sexpot effect, she added long, lustrous dark nylons and a pink frilly garter-belt. Soft-soled but high-heeled black boots completed her costume.

With her alligator bag slung over her shoulder, she went up by elevator to the green-jungled penthouse conservatory and out through sliding glass doors to the

11

roof of the apartment building. It was a high enough vantage point from which to see for several blocks.

The Dark Angel took from her bag the beautiful little ten-power electronically intensified night glasses specially crafted for her by Kensui of Tokyo. The nearest phone booth was on the corner of Third Avenue, a block and a half away. A brunette in a sleek red pant-suit came gradually into focus. She was standing in the window glow from the drugstore—obviously keeping her eye peeled toward the brightly lit, canopied entrance of the Turtle Bay Towers, waiting for Angela Harpe to show.

The night glasses went back into Angie's bag, and out came a small plastic pouch, from which Angie extracted her hooked nylon-cable climbing rig. With this she descended easily to the roof of the adjoining building, and from there scampered down a fire escape to an alleyway in back.

Debouching onto Second Avenue, Angie circled a four-block rectangle in order to approach her red-suited caller from precisely the opposite direction that she was expecting. Angie's silent footsteps took the brunette by surprise. She whirled at the sound of a voice over her shoulder.

"Hiya, Blondie," said the Dark Angel. "What're you? Some kind of quick-change artist? I mean, what's with that black hair dye? And who swiped your blue frock?"

The brunette's mouth opened and closed wordlessly as she stared at Angela Harpe. Finally she got hold of her voice. Forcing a smile which Angie found only semi-bewitching, she replied disarmingly, "Since you've found me out, I suppose I'd better confess—I never did believe in dealing face up."

"I'm sure. Still and all, baby, that was pretty stupid, wasn't it? You might've expected I'd check the desk clerk in the lobby."

12

"Yes, I guess that *was* a rather silly oversight—especially in dealing with someone as hip and cool as the Dark Angel. But you see, I was only trying to protect myself in case you didn't trust me. I was afraid you might call out some hardcase types to—I believe the street expression is 'work me over'?"

"Don't hand me that Junior League crap," said Angie mildly. "Let's face it. You know the streets as well as the next chippie. What you really mean is you wanted to take *me* by surprise, while I was still gawking around for a blonde in blue."

Even without the flickering movement of the brunette's eyes as a warning, Angie could see the man coming up behind her by his reflection in the drugstore window. She dropped her left shoulder so the strap of her alligator bag slid swiftly down into her hand. In the next instant she was swinging the bag behind her in a lightning reflex. There was an inch-thick steel bar in its bottom lining which, swung at arm's length, took on the striking force of a small sledge hammer.

The blow caught the man on the side of the head and laid him out cold on the pavement. He was a pug-faced, swarthy-skinned Oriental, with long dark hair slicked back over a bullet head. Angie filed him as half black, half Chinese, or what the Jamaicans call a Chigro. But there was only time for a quick glance before her eyes flashed back to the brunette scrabbling hastily in her patent-leather purse.

Angie's hand stopped her in the act. "Don't make it worse by going for a gun, baby—unless you want a broken wrist. Just tell me where to find this so-called principal of yours, and I'll let you off in one piece."

The brunette bit her lip in pain and gestured with her head toward the street. A long black Cadillac "Undertaker's Special" was just pulling up to the curb.

Angie yanked a small nickel-plated Belgian FN automatic out of the brunette's purse, emptied the magazine and sent gun and ammo spinning across the pavement. Then she turned and walked toward the Cadillac.

Its door opened at her approach, and a man wearing a black skull cap and half mask, like a medieval Jack Ketch executioner's disguise, looked out at her.

"Please get in, Miss Harpe. I assure you you're in no danger."

"Too right, I'm in no danger, honkie—but you are!" A pearl-handled Baby Browning had suddenly appeared in Angie's right hand.

The masked man's thin lips shaped a smile, and he nodded his head slowly in acceptance of her statement. "Of course, my dear. But my invitation still stands."

His English was precise—a trifle too precise for a native-born American—yet colored by a faint trace of accent which Angie couldn't place.

She returned his grin in spite of herself, climbed aboard and took her place on the back seat beside him. A thick pane of glass walled them off from the chauffeur's compartment. The masked man reached forward to press a button on an electronic control console just below the pane. The curbside door closed automatically and the Caddy glided off down the street.

"Allow me to apologize, Miss Harpe, for the stupid tactics of my subordinates."

The masked man's hands were gloved and his hair, or lack of it, was concealed by the skull cap-mask. But from his voice and the ravaged lines of his throat, Angie realized she was dealing with an old man—probably somewhere in his seventies.

"My secretary, Miss Nightgrove," he went on, "wrongly persuaded me that you might balk at a conversation with a sinister-looking masked man in an equally

14

sinister-looking car. Hence the idiotic attempt at force —which I was happy to see you disposed of in short order."

He chuckled quietly to himself. Or perhaps whinnied was more like it, Angie decided.

"Since you raised the subject, just why *are* you wearing a mask?" she inquired.

"I shall come to that in a moment, my dear. . . ." His voice trailed off into silence, and she saw that he was studying her in the lambent gloom, illuminated by the intermittent radiance of street lights as the car tooled along.

He himself seemed utterly unaware of, or indifferent to, anything odd about his wearing a mask. But then the Caddy's wide quarter panels and louvred rear windows, she realized, kept them both out of view by passing motorists or pedestrians.

"You're a very shapely young woman, Miss Harpe," he murmured. "Very well endowed, one might say."

"Speaking as an ass man, leg man or tit man?"

He cackled quietly. It was definitely a cackle this time. "Speaking as all three, by God—if you must fish for compliments. But let me add in frankness, my dear, that at my age I am forced to operate mostly as a tit man."

He eyed her in silence again for a moment or two before venturing, "For another thousand dollars, Miss Harpe, would you allow me to kiss and fondle your breasts?"

Angie chuckled back at him. "I think not, daddy. Since you've contacted me, you must know who I am and something about my background. Which means you probably know that besides fashion modeling, I also worked as a call girl, after my scholarship days at Radcliffe, in order to accumulate a stake for my future career as a private detective."

15

The masked man nodded. "I had reports to that effect."

"Well, it's true. And mind you, I'm not saying I didn't enjoy quite a lot of my tricks. For that matter, plenty of whites have thrived on black titty. But the point is, I quit selling it some time ago—and I'm not exactly tempted to go back into that line of business."

"Of course, of course. I quite understand, my dear." He paused thoughtfully. "On the other hand, at my age, one doesn't come in contact with too many morsels like you. So forgive me if I ask an impertinent question. . . . Are you wearing panties, Miss Harpe?"

"Matter of fact, I am. I had to come down a fire escape and—well, I thought the night might be a bit breezy."

"I'm so glad. If you won't allow me to caress your breasts, would you consider selling me your underpants for a thousand dollars?"

Angie burst out laughing. "Be my guest, daddy." She raised her hips, hiked up her mini-skirt and peeled off her tiny blue lace nylon bikini. "Bit skimpy on quantity, I'm afraid," she added, handing it over.

"Perfection, my dear! But do allow me to pay . . ." His wallet was already out.

"I'll put it on the bill," she giggled.

The masked man held up the panties in front of his face and pressed the crotch to his nose. "Ah, the intoxicating fragrance of womanhood," he murmured, inhaling deeply. "So much more romantic than mere perfume."

Angie watched with a tolerant smile. "As Omar Khayyam might have put it, 'What are all the perfumes of Araby, compared to one aromatic Persian pussy,' huh?"

The masked man broke up completely, cackling and wheezing. "I like you, my dear," he said when he finally

16

recovered his breath. "I do, indeed, like you. And I shall always treasure this precious memento. . . ." Once again he dangled the blue bikini in front of his face and sniffed.

"But enough of these digressions, however pleasurable. Let us proceed to business. . . . Miss Harpe, I would like you to undertake a rather dangerous assignment."

Chapter Two

"How dangerous?" Angie asked.

"Not *physically* dangerous. Or at least not terribly so. But illegal. Dangerous in the sense that you might get into serious trouble if caught. You see, the job involves breaking and entering."

"Breaking and entering what?"

"Somebody's room—or suite, rather," said her elderly client. "At an apartment hotel. To be specific, the Hotel Thermidor on West 38th Street."

"For what purpose?"

"To see if the owner has a certain something in his possession. Let me emphasize, by the way, that you will not be required to remove or steal anything—but merely to see if the item in question is there. And, if so, to photograph the evidence."

Angie was intrigued. "And what might this item be?"

The masked man pressed her panties to his nose while his hooded eyes regarded her thoughtfully. "One hesitates to be more specific . . . until one knows whether or not you will accept the assignment."

It was the Dark Angel's turn to hesitate. But only fractionally. Then she shrugged. "Let's say at this moment I'm inclined to give it a whirl. But nothing more

18

than inclined, however, until I know further details."

"Fair enough. I'm referring to an oil map—or maps. You know what that term means?"

Angie said, "I suppose it means some sort of map prepared by a geologist or prospecting team, showing where oil is located."

The masked man nodded. "Quite right. Which is enough to apprise you of the fact that we are playing for very large stakes indeed."

Angie felt a surge of adrenalin revving up her heartbeat. She glanced away, out the door window, to conceal the pleasurable tingle of excitement coursing through her. All in all, it sounded just the sort of job her body chemistry had been hungering for—but one must never let a client sense one's eagerness.

The car had been driving crosstown and was now, she noticed, coming down Broadway through the theater district.

Turning back, she said, "Why should I snoop at somebody else's oil map?"

"The map or maps," said the masked man, "happen to be mine. That is, if it or they exist."

"How can they be yours, if you don't even know whether or not they exist?" Angie asked sharply.

"Let me explain. This person at the Hotel Thermidor is a man named Laidlaw Pike, who might be variously described as an oil promoter, oil speculator, oil wildcatter or oil prospector. At one time or other, he's been all four, but more recently he's been somewhat down on his luck. Six months ago, I hired him to lead a prospecting team into a certain remote area of Colombia, South America."

"Any luck?"

"That, to paraphrase Hamlet, is the question."

The fuel crisis had dimmed the glitter of Times Square—if glitter was quite the word—but the hippies

19

and muggers and even the out-of-towners, it seemed, were still out there in full force.

"You see," the masked man went on, "when Pike came back from South America, he reported that the expedition had been completely unsuccessful. He had found no promising new oil sites whatever."

Angie said, "But I take it you have reason to doubt his word?"

"More than doubt. I'm convinced he's a damned liar."

"Why?"

"Because he's now in New York engaged in top-secret negotiations with the Staroleum Corporation."

"Hmm, I dig," murmured the Dark Angel. "In other words, you suspect he's about to peddle the data you paid him to find to another buyer."

"Precisely."

"Even if you're right, Pike must know he's playing a dangerous game. Realistically, what makes you think he'd keep such a map or maps in his hotel room?"

"Because it appears there's nowhere else they *can* be," retorted the masked man. "From certain reports reaching my ears, I began to suspect that Pike might not be trustworthy shortly before he returned to this country. I therefore had my agents keep him under surveillance from the time he landed in Houston. Now, in view of the present haphazard state of the U.S. Postal Service, I hardly think he'd be idiot enough to trust such valuable stuff to the mails. But it also happens that he has had no opportunity to deposit the maps in a bank vault or any other place of safekeeping—nor, as far as can be ascertained, to slip them to any other person."

"What if he keeps them on his own person?" said Angie.

"That, too, can be ruled out. While in Houston, Pike

20

visited a turkish bath, where my agents succeeded in going through his clothes. They found nothing."

"And you've had him watched since he arrived in New York?"

"Correct. He flew here from Houston several days ago."

Angie mused thoughtfully. "The Thermidor is an apartment hotel, as you mentioned. Does Pike always stay there when he's in New York?"

"Yes, always. In fact he maintains a more or less permanent suite there—except when he's out of town for long periods of time, as during this recent prospecting expedition. Even so, when he returns, they usually arrange for him to have the same quarters—715."

"I see. And suppose I search his suite and report back to you that I found no oil map. How will you know if I'm telling the truth—that I didn't find such a map and keep it myself?"

"Because, my dear," said the masked man drily, "I have already had you checked out—on both sides of the Atlantic. The Banque Nationale de Suisse in Geneva, Lloyds of London and a certain major insurance underwriting firm here in the States with which I do a great deal of business all assure me that your word can be trusted implicitly. These institutions do not make such judgments lightly or superficially. Besides, it would be most unwise of you to try to deceive me."

His last sentence was spoken in the mildest, most matter of fact tones. Nevertheless, it sounded extremely convincing to Angie.

"And what if I *do* find an oil map in Pike's suite?"

"What happens after that need not concern you, my dear." The old man chuckled. "Rest assured I shall take the matter from there."

Angela Harpe had grown up in the festering Harlem

21

slums—had plied her trade as a call girl in the deadly world of black pimps and white vice lords—had dealt with thieves, perverts, pushers, killers and equally deadly rogue cops during her stint on the NYPD—and had faced death a score of times since embarking on her career as a private eye.

But when the elderly dude in the black executioner's mask chuckled, her blood ran cold.

He smelled her blue bikini panties again, like a French courtier sniffing a pomander ball, and eyed her expectantly. "Well, Miss Harpe? Have you reached a decision yet on whether or not you will take the assignment?"

"I'll think it over and let you know in twenty-four hours."

"I'm afraid that won't do, Miss Harpe. I must know now."

"Okay, groovy. There are a few things I'd like to know, too," snapped Angie. "Like who the hell are you?"

"Ah, that I grant you is a trifle unfair. But I fear it's absolutely imperative that I withhold my identity."

"Imperative for whom?"

"For me and my business interests. The fact is that I am not publicly known to be in the United States at this time. And must not be. Even most of my closest subordinates are unaware of my presence back in the country at this moment. Were such news to leak out, it could result in the most violent financial repercussions."

"I see."

The old man's thin lips sketched the thinnest of smiles—like a microtome paring human tissue. "And by the way, Miss Harpe—if you have already noted the license plate number of this car, or intend to do so, pray don't bother. It is a practice of mine to have my car plates switched whenever I wish to safeguard my anonymity. I might add that a certain corrupt employee of the state's Motor Vehicle Bureau is paid handsomely to alert me whenever any attempt is made to trace one of my false license numbers."

Angie's growing desire to tell the old fart to go to hell struggled with an equally intense and feminine yen to pry more deeply into his affairs.

"There is another reason for urgency," the masked man went on. "My agents have informed me that Laidlaw Pike left the Hotel Thermidor at around eight o'clock tonight and is not expected to return before midnight. Thus, if you accept the assignment now, you will have almost three hours to search Pike's suite. Which is none too long for a really thorough search—but then you are an expert in such matters, which is another reason for hiring you."

Slowly, with an old man's deliberateness, he extracted a thickly stuffed wallet from his inner coat pocket and began to fan out hundred dollar bills.

"I am prepared to pay you twenty-five hundred dollars here and now, plus another twenty-five hundred when you report the results of your search tomorrow."

"For information on an oil strike that might be worth millions?" Angie laughed scornfully. "Horseshit, daddy. If I take the job, it'll cost you five Gs now, another five Gs when I report tomorrow—negative or affirmative—plus an extra ten grand for the film and/or steering you to the maps."

"Twenty thousand altogether—in the event of a successful conclusion?"

"Right on—you add real good."

"Agreed."

Thoughtfully Angie stuffed the twenty-five C-notes which he counted out into her shoulder bag—followed by a loaded Minox camera.

The masked man, meanwhile, flicked on his intercom

to the chauffeur. "The Hotel Thermidor on West 38th. Drive past it and stop at the next corner."

"Yes, sir."

"I am delighted to have obtained your services, Miss Harpe," said the old man, turning back to Angie. "May I, as the Viennese say, *küss die Hand?*"

She held out her hand and he pressed his lips to it gravely.

"When and how do I report?" she asked.

"You will hear from me before noon tomorrow."

They drove on in silence until the car stopped and Angie got out. The last thing she saw as the Cadillac pulled away was her blue panties being waved at her.

Angela grinned to herself. *Have to be careful I don't catch cold!*

She crossed the street and circled the block in order to enter by the Thermidor's side door, which was just around the corner from the main entrance, thus avoiding the doorman's scrutiny.

The lobby was busy—a stroke of luck, in spite of which she made a sharp-eyed visual reconnaissance for the hotel dick. Apparently he was busy topside or off-duty or taking a leak, because there was no one in sight who seemed to fill the bill. Her other big hazard was the bell captain. With her sexy figure and her micromini revealing her stocking tops practically every time she moved her legs, Angie knew her appearance was inflammatory to say the least. Given her druthers, she would have preferred to return to the Turtle Towers and garb herself more modestly before attempting the Thermidor job. But with only three hours available, minutes were too precious to waste. Anyhow, she knew all too well from past experience that a black fox like herself always drew calculating glances from hotel personnel, no matter what the hell she wore.

Angie waited at the side of the lobby till the slick-haired, cold-eyed bell captain was engrossed in conversation with a tourist couple. Then she walked quickly to the nearest self-service elevator not in use, buzzed the door shut and rode up to the ninth floor. From there, she walked two flights down the fire stairs to seven.

Aside from a fat man who gave her a frankly interested look on his way to the elevator, the corridor was empty. But voices and the sounds of television made it clear that the floor was alive with guests.

Suite 715 was located in a short, dead-end turnoff with only three other doors, which was both a break and a hazard. A break in that it minimized the likelihood of interruption. A hazard, heightened by the soft floor carpeting, in that she'd have little or no visual forewarning of anyone approaching—and no escape route if that person entered the turnoff.

However, Angie always carried in her bag a fake, plastic-tagged hotel key which she could use as emergency camouflage in such a crisis, pretending to discover that she'd gotten off at the wrong floor when she found the key didn't fit. She also carried a plastic-handled nail file and a gold-cylindered lipstick, both of which contained secret picklock devices. As it turned out, the door lock of 715 was no gimcrack to be "loided" open easily with a plastic credit card. But in little more than a minute it yielded to Angie's tools and skill.

She entered, closed the door softly behind her and stood listening in the dark for a moment before flicking on her flashlight. She was in the sitting room of Pike's suite. An archway on each side led to what was evidently a kitchen and dinette on the left, and a bedroom and bath on the right.

Better make sure the joint's empty first, thought Angie. Guided by her flashlight beam, she checked every

25

room. The window drapes had already been drawn—presumably by Laidlaw Pike before he left for the evening.

Angie parted one set of drapes enough to open the window and crane her head out—checking in all directions, up, down and sideways, for a possible escape route in case of emergency. Tough T, baby. A sheer drop. The only alternative would be to claw one's way up the shallow interstices in the stone siding for three stories to a parapet just above the tenth floor. Angie was a skilled gymnast, expertly trained in the techniques of cat burglary—but even with her nylon rig, she'd be risking her neck to tackle such an ascent. Fuck that noise, thought Angie. If she got interrupted, she'd just have to talk fast or figure some other way out.

Hopefully, if the masked man's agents were still tailing Pike, they might find some way to warn her if he returned unexpectedly. Still, it wasn't the sort of thing a smart gonif should count on, Angie cautioned herself.

Putting all such disturbing thoughts firmly out of her mind, Angie shut the window, drew the drapes again and switched on the sitting room light. She glanced around, sizing up the job that lay ahead. Jesus, she'd really have to work fast.

It occured to her that she'd neglected to ask how big an oil map might be. Still, that probably meant nothing, since it might have been photographically reduced or folded into a smaller size.

Following her usual rule, Angie began by looking in the most obvious place—in this case the writing desk in the sitting room. A swift three-and-a-half minute check convinced her it held no map and had no secret compartment.

Okay, next to the bedroom—with a peek in the closet first. The peek disclosed three suits, a topcoat-raincoat, some soiled shirts, socks and skivvies waiting to be laundered, a couple of pairs of shoes and engineer's boots and two empty suitcases. From all appearances, Pike wasn't a man who wasted much time or money on clothes.

Since the suitcases were empty, everything else must have been transferred to drawers. But wait a sec—what about that trunk near the foot of the bed? Angie discovered at once that it was locked. And heavily loaded.

Well, well, she thought, what have we here?

The lock opened after a few expert surgical probes with her nail file scalpel. Angie lifted the lid—and immediately wished she hadn't.

There was a girl inside.

Chapter Three

The girl was lying on her left side with her legs drawn up in the fetal position. She had long dark red hair and was clad in panties, bra and stockings. And she was very still and cold to the touch.

Angie turned away and leaned against the bed for a moment, trying to steady her nerves and her heaving stomach. Jesus H. Christ! What had she gotten herself into this time? Already, even at this early stage of the search, her fucking fingerprints were all over the joint!

She forced herself to look back into the trunk. And did her second double-take of the evening.

What the hell!

There was something odd about this chick. Wasn't her skin a little too smooth and hairless? Angie aimed her flashlight down into the trunk and fingered through the girl's titian locks to examine the hair roots. They looked suspicious, all right, but it was hard to tell for sure.

What about rigor mortis? Angie took hold of the girl's elbow to try to lift it. The upper arm raised easily from the shoulder—and stayed in its raised position. Likewise the forearm levered outward from the elbow—and remained extended. Scarcely believing her own eyes, Angie folded the arm up again and tucked it neatly back to the girl's side.

The girl's eyelids also retracted neatly but not quite humanly.

"Well, I'll be a blue-balled bitch!" muttered Angie, comforted by the sound of her own voice. The thing in the trunk was a goddamn, mother-fucking dummy! With jointed limbs encased in simulated plastic flesh.

Angie's own heart was still beating nineteen to the dozen. She slammed down the lid in a burst of petulance and relocked it, angry at Laidlaw Pike for keeping such a sick gadget and at herself for getting so upset. There was too much to be done to waste any more time on it.

Next to be checked was the chest of drawers and dresser. Each individual drawer was swiftly searched, then removed and inspected on all sides and underneath. The interior and rear surfaces of both chest and dresser were likewise examined.

Angie took the bedding apart and went over the pillows and mattress. None showed the slightest sign of having been ripped open and resewn. She checked the bed itself thoroughly for possible hollow spaces or crevices into which a paper map might have been inserted.

The minutes flew by as she worked her way methodically through the bedroom. Then the bathroom. Medicine cabinet, toilet, sink, shower enclosure, towel racks, overhead access paneling to the electrical, plumbing and air conditioning connections.

Back to the living room. Sofa, chairs, one by one. Take out cushions. Examine upholstery, bottom webbing, wooden members. Drawers, surfaces and joints of end table and occasional table. Bases and shades of lamps. Look behind wall mirror, check the backing. Ditto for two framed pictures. Remove back cover of television set and probe the dusty innards.

She was working at top speed now, smoothly and instinctively, with periodic glances at her watch to monitor the time. Into the search went every bit of expertise gleaned on umpteen earlier occasions of "turning over" a suspect's pad—almost always surreptitiously, without a warrant.

Going through the dinette and kitchen was the most boring part of the job—even depressing. Pike was obviously the kind of cook whose modus operandi ran to opening cans and heating frozen TV dinners, when he ate at home at all. And he hadn't even been back from South America long enough to re-stamp his individual personality on the setup. Refrigerator, stove, appliances —*nada*. Cupboards and drawers skimpily furnished with tinny flatware and plates and crockery that looked like slabs of bathroom porcelain. *Nada* again. Angie even probed the sink's drain elbow.

Last came the floors and walls. There was wall-to-wall carpeting everywhere except in the kitchen, which had wall-to-wall linoleum, and the bathroom, which was tiled. Angie patiently checked along the baseboards for any places where the carpeting might have been pried up—then over the surface of all carpeting for patches or slits which might clue the way to floorboard hidey-holes. Finally a room-by-room tapping and scratching over every wall.

She ended her search wearily with a glance at the time—11:17. Damned if I haven't earned tonight's six grand, Angie thought—and tomorrow's five, too!

Still, she hated to lose out on that ten thousand buck bonus—if only because she hated to end any case with a baffled, blank-wall feeling.

Angie stood frowning, with one hand on her hip and the other rubbing her chin. The dummy. That weird goddamn dummy. What did it mean? There had to be some connection, there just had to. Otherwise it was too damned coincidental—running across an intriguing gim-

30

mick like that on a case which had already started out with a masked panty-sniffer and a missing oil map.

Wait a minute!

The glimmer of an idea was tickling the back of her brain when suddenly she heard a key scrape in the lock. Like lightning, Angie darted for the wall switch, flicked it off and raced into the bedroom. It was a silent mercury switch, and her footfalls were equally noiseless on the carpeting.

Luckily, she was sure no light had seeped out to betray her presence, because she had carefully noted on entering that the door was flush with the carpet.

Also luckily, Pike seemed to be having trouble finding the keyhole. Maybe he was coming back from a social evening, half sloshed—which would certainly ease Angie's own predicament.

She had doused the kitchen-dinette lights when she finished searching that area. The main bedroom light was still burning—but on second thought she killed that, too. And stood there in the dark, asking herself rhetorically—in the manner of Oliver Hardy propounding disaster to Stan Laurel—how the hell she was going to con her way out of this one.

The answer came to her just as she heard the door opening in the sitting room. She sank softly onto the bed, then rose loudly—to a squeaky chorus of bedsprings. One hand was already unzipping her mini-shift to the waist, while her other hand scooped up her magnificent unbra-ed breasts and protruded them nakedly—like a gunner's mate running out his forty-pounders from an open casemate to aim a broadside at an enemy frigate.

She saw a glow of brilliance from the archway as the light went on again in the sitting room.

Swaying voluptuously, with tities a-bobble, Angela Harpe went pussyfooting out to greet the returning ten-

31

ant—yawning and pretending to rub her eyes sleepily.
"Mr. Pike?"

He goggled at her incredulously, obviously seeking
and failing to grapple with the question of where this
sexy brown apparition had sprung from.

He looked younger than Angie had expected, although a full black beard made it hard to place his age
too precisely, and his skin was deeply tanned by tropic
suns.

His mouth worked spasmodically before emitting:
"Wh–Wh–Where the hell did you come from?"

"From the bedroom," Angie explained. "I guess I
must have fallen asleep waiting for you." Her simpering
voice was a creditable imitation of Marilyn Monroe's
perverted-little-girl-yearning-to-attract-a-rapist.

"B–B–But who are you? And how did you get in
here?"

"Oh. You mean how did I get in your room?" she responded innocently. "It was the bell captain. He thought
you might . . . well, you know. . . . He thought you
might want to . . . to fuck me." Angie burst into girlish
giggles, causing her bronze rose-tipped mammaries to
tremble deliciously.

"Well, he's wrong!" The comeback was fiercely emotional—almost explosive.

"But, Mr. Pike—please don't be mad! He just
thought you'd like to—"

"*I said he's wrong!* I don't want to fu—to have inter-
course with you. I don't even *know* you, for heaven's
sake! And besides—even though I have no prejudice
against Negroes and I do respect you people—interra-
cial copulation is disgusting and immoral! In fact it—
it's specifically forbidden in both the Old and New Tes-
taments!"

He's got to be putting me on, thought Angie—the
dude can't be serious! But she sensed instantly that he

32

was. Jesus Christ, this Laidlaw Pike must be some kind of Bible belt freak—and she had to run into the jerk! At a time like this!

He was rambling on wildly—raving, working himself up. "Hang it all, can't you understand that this kind of promiscuous hotel soliciting is a violation of the law? Both kinds of law—the laws of God and the laws of man! It's brutalizing and—and depraved! Don't you realize it's shocking to every normal, decent human being? And if that makes no difference to you, why, good Lord, th–th–think of the risk you run of catching and spreading some ghastly venereal disease!"

Next thing, the stupid bastard would be grabbing the phone and calling the bell captain. Then she'd really be up Shit Creek! All the same, Angie noticed he kept staring hypnotically at her bare bulging tits, the hypocritical sonofabitch. The thing to do was to keep his attention fixated.

She grabbed the zipper and yanked her mini-shift open all the way. Letting the dress slip from her shoulders, she stepped forth totally revealed—mother naked, except for her frilly pink garter belt and lustrous nylons and black high-heeled boots.

There, let the ofay bastard get a load of that!

He stopped short in mid-sentence and his mouth dropped open while his bug-eyed stare traveled slowly downward from her breasts to her belly-button to the crisp black thatch vee-ed between her long, shapely legs. Jesus, he was actually quivering.

Angie seized the initiative. She moved toward him, jiggling adorably at every step. With her one hand she took *his* hand and rubbed it over her tits, while her other hand unzipped his fly.

"F–F–For God's sake, young lady! Wh–Wh–What do you think you're doing?" he croaked.

"Preparing to stimulate you—orally," she murmured,

33

sinking to her knees and tugging down his slacks and shorts. His genital was already large and tumescent, and it stiffened with an almost audible *boing!* as she guided it between her lips.

"No! *No!*" he exclaimed. His voice had turned shrill. Grabbing Angie under the arms, he raised her back to her feet. But instead of shoving her away from him, he seemed to be hugging her closer. Her own arms stole around his neck.

Next thing Angie knew, they were toppling like felled timber and she was flat on her back and he was ramming it home with manic intensity. Her gartered, booted legs locked around the small of his back while he pumped up an ultimate liquid explosion that sent them both gushing seaward at high tide.

She saw Pike staring at her glassy-eyed, and she kissed him, and he went limp in her arms. Gently she extricated herself from underneath him and rose to her feet.

"I'm . . . not sure I . . . have enough c–c–cash . . . to pay you, Miss," he mumbled from somewhere around floor level.

"It's okay, honey," Angie assured him. "A screw that good can be on the house."

She pulled on and zipped up her mini-shift, grabbed her shoulder bag and got the hell out of 715.

Angela Harpe awoke next morning in her own luxurious pink-silk-sheeted bed when the alarm tinkled promptly at nine. She freshened up in the shower, dressed herself in gingham shorts with a matching halter and breakfasted on scramble eggs, toast and freshly ground coffee—the last cup of which she took with her to the phone.

High time to prime herself with a little info before the masked panty-sniffer called for her report. Part of the

34

Dark Angel's success as a private eye lay in her ability to tap expert sources of information fast.

Let's see, she mused, as she savored the rich, steamy mocha flavor from her cup—who's my best boy on oil?

Ah, yes! That brainy black dude at *Business World*. Scott Hogarth.

Angie looked up his number and dialed. He recognized her voice instantly.

"Hey, sugar! How you doing this bright and sunshiny morning?"

"Groovy, man. But I need some help. Can you lay a little information on me, Hogie?"

"Oh, I dare say something might be worked out along those lines . . . maybe tit for tat.

"Well, I don't mind slipping you some tit one of these days," said Angie, "but tat's not what I'm after. It's oil. How much can you tell me on that subject, brother?"

"Try me," said Hogarth with an air of modest confidence.

"Okay. Have to do it like charades, though. The guy I'm trying to identify is some kind of bigshot in the oil industry. Foreign born, but possibly a naturalized citizen now—at least he knows his way around the English language and probably spends a lot of time in this country. He's autocratic, loaded with dough, a bit of a mystery man and has a foxy brunette secretary who probably does more than answer his mail. The guy himself, I'd say, is somewhere in his seventies. And at the moment he's reported to be outside the country—"

"Don't bother going on, Mama. You've gotta be talking about Xerxes Zagrevi."

"*Xerxes Zagrevi!* Of course!" exclaimed Angie. "Now why the hell couldn't I think of that? Iranian, isn't he?"

"That's right. Head of the English-Zagrevi Oil Consortium, otherwise known as E-Z Oil. Spends his time

35

flitting between Teheran, London, New York and practically anywhere else you can point to on a map."

"Okay, next question. Where's the action in oil these days? I mean new strikes, new territories being opened up. . . ."

"Well, hell, lots of places," said Hogarth. "The North Sea, Indonesia, Alaska—you name it."

"Any down in Colombia?" asked Angie.

"Yeah, matter of fact that's quite a hot little scene right now—or so it's rumored."

"Has Zagrevi got a piece of the action down there?"

"No, but he'd probably like to."

"Who has?"

"Two operators, according to the word that's leaked out so far," replied Scott Hogarth. "One is Emerald Oil, which is a small American company, and the other's an independent—a promotor named Laidlaw Pike."

"Wait a minute," said Angie slowly. "You did say Pike's an independent?"

"That's right. He's reported to be dickering with Staroleum. Did you get the *New York Times* today, Mama?"

"Haven't read it yet," said Angie, "but it's probably lying right outside my door."

"Go bring it in," said Hogarth. "I'll hang on."

"Okay." Angie went off to the door to get the paper, which was delivered every morning to her and other subscribers in the building by one of the Turtle Towers employees. "Got it, Hogie," she reported.

"Good. Now turn to page 54 in the business section. You'll find a short interview there with Laidlaw Pike that tells the whole story." As he heard Angie turning the pages, Hogarth added, "Got it? In column two, headed 'New Oil Strike Reported in Colombia' . . . with a picture of Pike."

Angie's eyes swept the page. There was the story, all

right, and there was the picture captioned *Laidlaw Pike*. Only the man in the photo wasn't youngish and black-bearded—he was a gnarled, elderly gent with clean-shaven dewlaps.

Hogarth heard the Dark Angel gasp.

"What's the matter, baby?"

"Jesus, Hogie—I think I've been raped!"

Chapter Four

"Come again, Mama?" Scott Hogarth chuckled, "Or perhaps I should rephrase that. . . ."

"Don't bother. Let's just say I was led to believe that Laidlaw Pike was a young dude in his twenties or thirties with a black beard. According to this picture, he's a beat-up old roustabout with a caved-in face and jowls like a bloodhound."

"The picture's right, baby," said Hogarth. "I've seen him in the flesh. That old honkie's been around."

Angie's eyes hastily scanned the news item. The occasion for the *Times* interview was a talk on South American oil prospects given by Pike at last night's bimonthly meeting of the Petroleum Society—which incidentally, Angie realized, explained how Zagrevi had known Laidlaw Pike would be away from his hotel suite between eight o'clock and midnight.

"Look," she said into the phone. "This *Times* story reports that Pike has been exploring for oil on his own down in Colombia—and apparently he's found it."

"That's what it do say," Hogarth agreed.

"Could it be that his independent status is just windowdressing—in other words, pure jive—and that actually his exploration was secretly financed by one of the big oil outfits, like say Zagrevi's E-Z Oil Consortium?"

"I don't get you, Mama. If they backed him, why keep it secret?"

"Who knows? What I'm leading up to is this. Is there any chance that Pike might have gotten his original financing from some company like E-Z, and now he's double-crossing them by turning around and trying to peddle his prospect to Staroleum?"

Hogarth laughed. "No way, baby. No way."

"Why not?"

"For openers, it'd be practically impossible to keep a deal like that secret from the industry. Before Pike ever got back to the States, everyone in the trade would have known he was down there surveying for Zagrevi. For raisers, Pike's an old hand at the game. He wouldn't be stupid enough to try such a barefaced double-cross."

"Repeat—why not?"

"Reasons of health, baby. They play rough in the oil business. Like out in the field, when they're doing some test drilling, if they catch a scout for some rival outfit snooping around, man, they work him over. That cat's lucky if he doesn't get carted away in an ambulance—or a pine box. For a dude like Pike to try a bareass cheat would be like writing his own obituary." Scott Hogarth paused for breath.

"You see, Mama, these days it costs a lot more than peanuts to send out an oil prospecting expedition. Pike must have hocked himself to the eyeballs to raise the do-re-mi. He didn't just run an aerial survey or have surface geologists out tapping rocks. He went to seismic testing, gravity crews—the whole schmeer. And, baby, all that data would have to be fed back to whoever was paying for it. Or else. So as far as Pike working for some other company and double-crossing them goes—forget it."

Angie said thoughtfully. "Thanks for the fill-in, Hogie."

"If you liked *that* fill-in, baby, wait'll I show you an even better way I could do it."

Angie giggled. "Let's have lunch next week and you can draw me a picture."

Her grin lap-dissolved into anger as she hung up, her eyes blazing at the mental picture of Zagrevi in his mask —sniffing her panties while he fed her a load of con. That Persian prick! The Dark Angel didn't take kindly to clients who abused her trust—especially to someone who tried using her as a cat's-paw in what amounted to an out-and-out heist.

She shucked her gingham shorts and halter, and changed to a crisply revealing cotton madras pantsuit in bleeding blue batik. The phone rang just as she was about to leave for the office. As expected, it was an old man's voice at the other end of the line. *The* old man.

"Any luck, my dear?"

"I got into Pike's suite at the Hotel Thermidor, if that's what you're asking," said Angie. "I found no oil map."

"Ah. What a pity."

"However, it did occur to me afterward that there's still another place I might look."

She heard an eager hiss of indrawn breath. "I see." The old man chuckled drily, a trifle contemptuously. "In other words, you mean you're raising your price."

"I mean shit," said Angie coldly.

". . . I fear some of the nuances of today's slang expressions escape me, my dear."

"Then I'll spell it out. You and I are no longer doing business. The deal's off, Zagrevi."

There was a silence that lengthened with an increasingly chill air of menace. "So you have undertaken to

40

find out my identity—in direct disregard of my instructions."

"That's not all I've found out, honkie. I've also read this morning's *Times*."

"Ah! Suddenly I understand, Miss Harpe." Zagrevi's voice eased a notch. "That interview with Laidlaw Pike. You're upset because you've discovered he was, in fact, prospecting for oil in South America on his own, and not for my E-Z Oil Consortium."

"Now you're getting down," said Angie.

"Bear in mind, my dear, that there are five thousand dollars still to be paid you."

"You know what you can do with those five Gs, Zagrevi."

"And another ten thousand should your afterthought about the hiding place of the map prove correct."

"Shove it all."

"Twenty-five thousand."

"I'm no thief for hire, Zagrevi—especially by some lying bastard who ropes me into a sleazy second-story job."

"Rather strongly moralistic terms, surely, coming from a black ex-prostitute. Or should I simply use the *mot juste* and say—nigger whore?"

"Whose pants you begged to sniff? Yes, let's do please get earthy by all means—but some other time, if you don't mind. I'm afraid I can't waste any more of my morning exchanging pleasantries with old dribblers. . . . So long, Wog."

Angie put down the phone softly, breathing just a trifle harder than usual. A few deep breaths with her eyes closed, in the yoga lotus posture, soon corrected that. Going out through the lobby of the Turtle Bay Towers a few minutes later, she had the doorman flag her a cab. Angie rode south through the clangorous Manhattan traffic to East 42nd Street, where the taxi let her out in front of the building, near Grand Central Station, where she had her cozy little office.

This forenoon as she entered, however, her office seemed notably less cozy than usual. What detracted from its charm was a man with a gun. The gun was an Astra auto-pistol snouted with a big black cylindrical silencer, and it appeared to be aimed with businesslike intent somewhere between Angela Harpe's two tits.

Angie looked at the gun and at the man holding it. He was a sharp-looking white dude with a bushy black pseudo-Afro and luxuriant sideburns. He was wearing a wide-lapeled, wasp-waisted tan suit with a green windowpane check, a darker green turtlenecked jersey and a nasty sneer. He was standing in the doorway between the outer reception room and her inner private office—and from the view beyond, one gathered he had been ransacking her desk and file cabinets rather carelessly.

"Is this a business call, or personal?" said Angie.

"You can't hardly get much more personal than I'm gonna get, Mama," said the gunman. "Come on in all the way, and close that door to the hall."

Angie did.

"Now take off the top of your suit, dinge, and make it snappy."

"Fuck you, ofay."

"We may get around to that, if I like the looks of your ass. Ordinarily I don't soil my cock with dark meat, but you look like you might have a reasonably clean hole—as coon cunt goes, that is."

He lowered the aim of his Astra. There was a hollow thump—and a bullet hole appeared in the pink carpeting between Angie's feet.

"Move, nigger!"

Angie slowly lowered her shoulder bag to the floor and began unbuttoning the jacket of her pantsuit. Presently the jacket came off, revealing her generous brown pink-nippled breasts, heaped to overflowing on the half-cups of her white brassiere.

"Bra too, jig."

The brassiere came off.

The gunman came a few steps closer and slipped a hand into his coat pocket. It came out with a tightly rolled wad of black cloth impaled on two of his fingers. He gave a flip of his hand so that the wad unrolled, its free end snaking through the air in Angie's direction. She saw then that it was a long chiffon scarf or sash.

"Put the end of that in your mouth," he ordered. Angie complied. "Now start gobbling, nigger girl."

She fed the scarf into her mouth, bit by bit, salivating and wadding it tightly to keep from choking. By the time she had drawn in the last few inches, her mouth was tightly crammed with the material.

The gunman grinned and slipped his hand into another pocket. This time it came out with his fingers sheathed in a deadly looking, four-pronged metal claw. He held it up to show Angie. The talons extended well beyond his fingertips. Each was honed along it sides to razor-sharpness, and tapered to a curving stiletto point.

"Cute, huh?" The gunman tittered. Angela Harpe was not amused. Nor reassured when he added, "But don't get scared, Mama—I'm not gonna use 'em on you just yet. Not unless you give me any trouble."

He eyed her breasts greedily as he spoke. "Now turn around and lean against the wall. Arms wide and legs spread out, just like the fuckin' fuzz makes you do it."

Angie's brain was revving at top speed as she obeyed. What the hell was she going to do? This bastard was an obvious sado-freak—she could sense it from the vibes he gave off.

She heard him come up behind her, felt the hard muzzle of the silencer ram coldly against her back. His left hand slid over her shoulder, but it was no longer wearing the steel claw. Now it was holding a rectangular piece of tape, which he proceeded to plaster tightly over her lips.

Goddammit, he had her gagged for keeps now. There went any lingering chance she might have had of yelling for help.

"You can straighten up and turn around now—but do it slow and cool like the man tells you."

Angie followed orders. He reached out and aimed the Astra auto-pistol into her belly-button. Then his other hand slipped on the steel claw again and raked it gently across her bulging right titty. The stiletto-sharp talons left four fine red lines on her bronze skin.

The gunman chuckled with deep-down amusement. Angela Harpe showed no pain and watched him coolly —but hell's fury was raging inside her head. She was going to fix this creep. It was just a matter of waiting and watching for the right moment, that was all. Like a stalking tigress.

"Drop your pants, honey. And I do mean *drop* 'em —just in case you've got any smartass ideas about peeling 'em off and slinging 'em at me."

He backed away cautiously a step or two. Angie unzipped her hiphangers and half pushed, half wriggled them down over her buns till they fell in a heap around her ankles. The gunman leered at her white panties, which were little more than a G-string.

"Those too, baby."

Angie stripped all the way.

"Now down on the floor, nigger girl. Flat on your back and spread your legs. . . . . Tha—a—at's right. Hey now, that's quite a pussy you got there." He stared down avidly at the crisp black fur around her slot. "Yeah, man! I'd say that looks good enough to take a plunge. Probably creaming for me already, huh?"

44

He waved his clawed hand. "Tell you what. You gimme a good ride and I won't use these too hard on you. But make it good now, hear?—or I may have to stripe your face."

The creep removed his claw and shrugged off his coat, one sleeve at a time, transferring the gun from his right hand to his left as he did so. He undid his fly and took out his cock, which was already stiffly engorged. The gun went back to his right hand, and the claw went back on his left.

Another chuckle. "Ready or not I'm coming, baby!"

Angie's legs were spread and her knees were drawn up to receive him. He was halfway down on his knees when she let him have it. Her left leg suddenly straightened in a vicious kick that caught him squarely under the chin. He reeled back, triggering the gun by reflex. The bullet plowed into the carpet where Angie had been lying a split second earlier, before she rolled clear. Her hand reached out for her shoulder bag. Grabbing it by the strap, she swung it in a smashing arc. Its steel-bar-weighted frame slammed into his head with stunning force.

Angie sprang to her feet while he was still dazed and witless, squeezing off shots blindly. Another kick sent the gun flying from his hand. He lashed out with the steel claw and Angie kicked again, this time drawing a screech of pain. His face went sickly white and his arm dangled limply. She gave him another belt with her bag —only a glancing blow, but hard enough to send him sprawling forward on his face.

Angie went for the gun. But Afro Boy had lost all heart for further combat. He came off the deck dizzily but at panic speed, snatching up his coat and lunging wildly toward the exit.

Angie shot him in the leg just as he went out the door. He gasped and staggered but kept going. She knew she had nailed him, however, if only a flesh wound in the thigh.

She darted toward the door and yanked it open. The creep was racing frantically down the hall.

Just as he disappeared around the corner, Angie shot him in the ass.

Chapter Five

Should she go after the bastard? The temptation was strong—especially since she'd nicked him in the thigh and the butt, which would sure as hell slow him down.

But stark naked, with her mouth taped? Fat fucking chance!

Even fully dressed, she could hardly hope to collar the creep without stirring up a public hassle—and some stupid shit calling the cops. Likely as not, she'd wind up with her cheesecake photo plastered across the front page of the New York *Daily News*—which in Angie's dangerous trade could be a disaster. The public at large and most of the underworld didn't even connect the Dark Angel with her modest little office in this building labeled *A. Harpe, Private Investigator*. And Angie preferred to keep it that way.

There was also the risk of getting busted for mayhem. Defending herself with undue force. It had actually happened to one poor chick in New York—charged and arrested for disabling her would-be rapist. *Sheee-yit!* Angie relieved her feelings by slamming the office door so hard the glass pane rattled.

She stalked into her private office and ripped the tape off her mouth. *Ouch!* No skin lost but it still stung like hell. Especially with negroid lips. Not that hers were particularly wide, or that she'd trade with any thin-lipped honkie.

Oh well . . . no use standing around bitching and feeling sorry for herself.

It looked as though Afro Boy had whetted his prelim-inary spite mostly by scattering the contents of her desk and file drawers in all directions, without taking time to tear up or destroy anything. Which at least simplified her clean-up job.

He might, of course, have been looking for some-thing. Interesting point. But what? Not much hope of finding out now.

Angie's first thought had been that Xerxes Zagrevi might have sent the creep. To teach her not to get smart with Persian oil biggies. But the timing was wrong. Even with a snap of his potent fingers, Zagrevi couldn't have planted a thug in her office between the time she hung up on him and the time she reached East 42nd by taxi. Not plausibly.

All the same, the motive still smelled like revenge—and Zagrevi sure as hell wasn't the only party who'd love to see the Dark Angel worked over. As she patient-ly and methodically gathered up her strewn office files, Angie winnowed a mental list of candidates.

"Er . . . Miss Harpe."

Had Angie been a cat, she would have leaped a yard in the air. Being herself, she whirled and the Astra auto-matic leaped into her hand in a 0.9 second reaction. When the voice spoke, she'd been hunkering down gath-ering papers off the floor, with her bare ass aimed to-ward the doorway into the outer office.

Now, as she rotated swiftly upright, she saw the speaker. And did an incredulous "make." It was the black-bearded dude she'd had sexual congress with the

48

night before in Laidlaw Pike's hotel suite! Only now he was minus the beard—but his identity was unmistakable.

"You've got a fucking nerve!" Angie exploded.

Her visitor hastily averted his eyes. "B–B–Believe me, Miss Harpe, I don't *mean* to keep barging in when you're in such a—an exposed condition."

"Never mind my goddamned condition!" snapped Angie. Nevertheless, realizing her nudity, she added, "Turn around, Klutz. And keep your mitts up where I can see them."

Retrieving her clothes, she put them on fast, then frisked her visitor—repressing a momentary inclination, as her hands slid south of his belt, to take a passing feel of his genitals.

"Okay, turn around again. Now what the hell do *you* want?"

He met her eyes with an embarrassed but quite serious expression. "Your help, Miss Harpe."

"My *help*? Jesus Christ, you got a free piece last night, practically served up on a silver platter and spoon fed! What more do you want? A course of ten easy lessons?"

The young man (Angie sized him without the beard as twenty-seven at most) laughed awkwardly. Even a trifle nervously. "I guess I've got some explaining to do, all right."

"You can start with your name," said Angie. "And while you're at it, come on in here." She led the way into her private office. "Still a bit disordered, as you see I had another visitor before you showed. I walked in and found him raiding my files. Things got a bit rough. That's why I was straightening up."

The young man stared around the room, then back at Angie. "Good Lord! Can I help?"

"Forget it." As they took chairs, Angie switched on the tape recorder on her desk. "Let's go back to the name bit."

"Jack Bristol."

"Address?"

"Well, no fixed. At present I'm registered at the Warrick Plaza. Originally I came from California."

"What were you doing in Laidlaw Pike's hotel suite last night?"

"Looking for clues."

"Clues? To what?"

"Murder."

Angie took a deep breath, momentarily conscious of the same feeling that had swept over her when she found the redhead in Pike's trunk. "Somebody's been murdered?"

The young man nodded grimly. "My father, Lang Bristol. About eight months ago."

Angie relaxed imperceptibly and settled back in her chair. "This is what you want me to help you with?"

"That's right—to find his killer."

"Okay. I'm listening." As he started to speak, Angie interrupted with a sudden wave of her hand. "No, wait! First tell me how you located me here."

"Oh. Well. Last night I saw your face—"

"I'm surprised you noticed."

Jack Bristol flushed beneath his tropic tan. "Miss Harpe, I truly apologize for wh—"

"Never mind that jive. Stick to the point."

"Well, after I got back to my hotel," Bristol explained, "I happened to be looking through a magazine before I turned in. It had this article about a flock of art thefts on the Riviera last summer, and how the insurance underwriters had called in a female private eye known as the Dark Angel to help recover the loot.

There was a picture of her—not very good, just blown up from a snapshot—but anyhow, I realized the girl in the photo was *you*. The same girl I'd just—I mean, the girl I'd seen in Pike's hotel suite."

"The Dark Angel wasn't publicly *named* in that case," Angie pointed out. "Or in the magazine article, either."

"You mean, named as Miss Angela Harpe? No, that's true. But you see I have this friend who's a well-known oil executive. He checked with the insurance underwriters, and they told him to try a private investigator at this address."

Angie nodded. "Okay. Now back to the murder."

Bristol's youthful face hardened. "My father's name was Lang Bristol. He was a petroleum geologist employed by the Emerald Oil Company."

"Located where?"

"The company? Their operating headquarters is down in Houston. But like most other outfits, they also have a front office here in Manhattan."

"I dig. Go on."

"Well, as I say, my father was murdered about eight months ago. Last October thirty-first, to be precise. He was found shot to death on a farm in upstate New York. Or rather, not a farm exactly, but rural at least—sort of a country house—a very pleasant old place that Dad owned. He used to rest up there when he was on leave from his oil job. Anyhow, the setting isn't important."

"Why not?" asked Angie.

Jack Bristol said, "Because his killing wasn't a local crime, I'm sure of that. Dad was sort of a lone wolf type, you see. He had no particular friends or ties in the area. To him it was just a place to loaf and rest up between boozing forays down among the bright lights. From all indications, the murder was a professional job.

There were no signs of a struggle or any kind of violence. Nothing stolen. The bullet just came through an open window. Drilled him right between the eyes."

"You have any idea of who might've wanted him out of the way? I mean, enough to hire a professional hit man."

Bristol shook his head. "Not really. But there's another reason why I'm sure it wasn't a local crime."

"Like what?"

"A very odd situation had developed. Dad had just returned from an oil prospecting expedition in South America. The official report was that the expedition had been a failure—they'd found nothing. Yet almost immediately afterward, a rumor began to spread that the company had made a big strike—was maybe on the verge of opening up a major new oilfield. Well naturally, when you stir up a smell of big money like that, it's bound to bring out all the hungry wolves in the industry. And Dad was sitting right on top of the meat pile. He was the company's chief geologist. If there was any inside information for sale, Lang Bristol was the guy who'd have it. And that's when he got shot."

"You think your father *might* have sold any inside information?" said Angie without beating around the bush.

"Not a chance," Jack Bristol said stiffly. "Dad was a company man. He'd worked for Emerald Oil almost thirty years—ever since he got out of the army after World War II. He and the company's board chairman, Fergus Doyle, were close personal friends. So why would he start playing Judas? Money meant nothing to Dad, anyhow."

Angie eyed her visitor thoughtfully, noting his light-colored gabardine suit, dark brown shirt and neat knit tie. No fashion plate, but a good-looking dude with his crisp black locks and healthy tan. Western-outdoorsy type. With Bible Belt overtones. Out loud she said, "That rumor about Emerald Oil making a South American strike—it's still going around, I believe."

"That's right," agreed Bristol, "but the company also had another prospecting expedition out in the field last winter. Matter of fact I was on it. Down in Colombia."

Angie frowned. "You're an employee of Emerald Oil, too?"

"Well, for the moment—yes. Actually I'm a research chemist. I work for an industrial chemical firm out on the coast—or at least I did. They gave me leave to come East when my father was killed. Then later on I quit for good . . . to try to run down his killer."

"You haven't mentioned your mother."

"She's dead." Jack Bristol's eyes shifted momentarily from the Dark Angel. "Mother and Dad were divorced back in the 1950s when I was still a kid. She took me back to California, where she'd come from—and after she died in 1960, I was raised by my grandparents in Fresno. But they're dead now, too."

"They didn't approve of your father?"

Bristol's teeth showed whitely against his dark tan. "How did you guess? No, they never approved of Dad's drinking—and what they called his loose ways. I didn't see too much of him over the years. But he always sent my support money regularly—and presents for my birthday and at Christmas. And he paid my way through CalTech—including two years for my master's degree."

"So you decided to find his killer."

Jack Bristol nodded. "I felt I owed him that much. Especially since the police were doing nothing. They'd obviously written his case off."

Angela Harpe got up absent-mindedly from her pink leather chair to retrieve the scattered contents of a file folder from the floor near her carved teakwood desk—not wholly unaware, as she squatted to gather up the papers, that her thin cotton pantsuit beautifully showed off her swelling curves.

"How exactly did you hope to find your father's killer?"

"Well, for a start, I went to see Fergus Doyle after the funeral. As I told you, he's the company's board chairman and an old friend of Dad's. He confirmed everything I'd already heard—I mean the rumors circulating about Emerald Oil, and Dad being sort of in a crossfire as the chief geologist. It turned out Doyle's just as convinced as I am that Dad's murder is connected with the oil business."

"Has he offered any theory?"

Bristol hesitated. "Not exactly. But I have a strange feeling he's got one—something he's holding back, as if he's afraid to put it into words or make any definite accusation. Somehow I get the impression he's hoping I'll either prove or disprove whatever notion's gnawing away in his mind."

The Dark Angel said, "Did you come right out and ask if the rumors are true—about Emerald Oil making a strike?"

"Yes, I did. He claimed they were hot air."

"You believe him?"

"Why not? It would be all to the company's advantage to make people believe there *was* a strike. It would send the company's stock soaring. Which is what's happening right now, as a matter of fact."

"I know," said Angie, tucking the folder away in the top file drawer. "I also noticed when you were telling me Doyle's answer that you used the past tense—*'claimed'*—as if he may have changed his tune."

"Well, all this was last fall, when I first came East after Dad's murder," Jack Bristol explained. "Since then another expedition's gone out. The picture could be completely different now. Maybe the company *has* made a strike."

Angie shut the drawer and picked up a piece of metal sculpture that Creepo had knocked off the file cabinet. Luckily undamaged, it was a glittering spiky abstraction that looked like a crazy chrome Christmas tree—each spike tipped by some oddment of colored glass or hunk of hardware gilded with metallic fluorescent paint. The opus had been created as a love token for Angie by Moses Tatum, an incredible blind mechanic in a Bed-Stuy garage who insisted he could "smell" colors.

"You say the picture could be different," she remarked, turning to face Bristol. "Forgive my asking if it's none of my business, but don't you *know* whether the company's made a strike? I thought you were just back from Emerald Oil's latest prospecting expedition."

"That's right, and I still don't know—dumb as that may sound. For one thing, we were under frequent surveillance by other companies' spies out in the field, so there was ultra-tight security. Nobody was supposed to discuss our daily reports with anybody—even among ourselves. I was working with a seismic team and spent most of my time planting what they call 'jugs.' "

"Not the corn likker variety?"

Jack Bristol grinned again. "Nope, detectors. They pick up the shock waves from our test blasts and transmit them to seismographs aboard a truck. Ever seen a seismograph reading on a strip of photographic paper?"

"Well—of a sort," said the Dark Angel. "The kind you see on TV whenever there's a report of an earthquake temblor."

"Same thing. Just a bunch of squiggly lines. And who knows what they mean, unless you're an expert studying the overall picture. In our case, all the field data was shot straight back to Houston for interpretation and evaluation. As far as the ordinary roughnecks and roust-abouts go, they mean zilch."

"Still and all—you must have picked up *some* general impression."

"Well . . . yes . . . I did." Bristol slowly ran his fingers through his black hair. "All right, if you want a guess, I'd say affirmative. My hunch is Emerald Oil hit big. But who knows?"

"Natch." Angie found herself enjoying the hard time young Jack Bristol was having keeping his eyes off her figure. Especially around the low-cut neckline of her suit and the gap of bare bronze skin beneath the bottom of her shorty jacket, which allowed her belly button to peep out so coyly above her pants top. And farther south, and even more especially, the snug fit of the madras around her crotch, molding so beautifully the grooved contour of her mound. "You still haven't told me why you went on this oil-prospecting expedition," she continued.

Jack shrugged awkwardly. "You've probably guessed it. I wanted to check out the possibility that Dad's killer might have been someone *inside* the company—proba-bly someone who'd been with him on the earlier expedi-tion. So Doyle fixed it up for me to go along."

"Incognito?"

"No, no—as Lang Bristol's son. All the guys I worked with assumed that Doyle and Axby—who's president of the company—were grooming me for a shove up the executive ladder. But of course I was hop-ing the killer, whoever he might be, would figure I was on his trail and get nervous and maybe give himself away."

"Any luck?"

"None. None at all. Oh, I picked up lots of informa-tion about Dad's working relationship with different people in the company. But nothing of any real importance. Apparently Dad was pretty popular on all levels. Everyone seems to remember him affectionately."

"So what're you doing now in New York?" asked Angela Harpe.

"Well, as you may have heard, Emerald Oil's become quite a hot property. Some of the bigger outfits are putting out feelers for a takeover."

"Including E-Z Oil?"

Jack Bristol shot her a curious glance. "Not that I know of—which doesn't prove anything. At the moment, the company's dickering with Staroleum. So Wagner Axby, who's president of Emerald, has brought a small key group of the company's executive and technical personnel East for what he calls some 'frank questioning' by the Staroleum people."

"And you're included in this key group?"

Bristol nodded. "Again, by courtesy of Fergus Doyle. The idea was that it might give me a chance to size up some other possible suspects—or at least get the feel of any cross-currents inside the company that might've had a bearing on Dad's death."

"And still no luck?"

"A total blank. The truth is, I'm no longer sure Dad's murder was an inside job."

"Meaning?"

"Oh, I'm still certain the killing was connected with oil. But now I'm inclined to think Dad was shot by someone *out*side the company—someone who either had, or was trying to pick up and peddle, some secret dope on Emerald's prospects."

"I see." Angie's voice was thoughtful, but a faint reminiscent smile flickered over her face. "Which no doubt explains your unannounced visit last night to Laidlaw Pike's hotel suite."

She broke off abruptly and strode into the reception room. Her eyes had just noticed a vague dark shadow through the frosted glass pane of her outer office door.

Angie started to yank the door open—then jerked back in fear as something whizzed audibly past her face. The whizz ended in a sharp *plunk!*

Even with the sound to guide her, it took Angie a moment to make out the long steel needle which had buried itself in the wall at her left.

Chapter Six

"What's wrong?" Jack Bristol had come up behind her while Angie stood there gasping.

She pointed wordlessly to the needle in the wall.

"Holy smoke!" He tried to pull it out. But the needle was evidently barbed and had driven itself so deeply through the plaster that it couldn't be extracted by hand. Even so, a good six inches of shaft protruded, with a flattened, slightly spatulate end.

"Never mind," said Angie. "I can always use it as a coat hook."

"You mean somebody actually tried to *shoot* you with this thing just now?" Bristol stared at her incredulously.

"What do you think? Some crochet freak just got carried away with enthusiasm?"

The dark shadow was long gone from the other side of the glass pane. Angie opened the door cautiously and glanced outside. "Hmm, looks like whoever did it also left a package. Maybe the needle's a new parcel-delivery come-on for female customers. Open the door and you get your ears pierced free."

She brought in a brown paper bag bearing a ten-cents-store marking. Inside the bag was a gold-colored, wire-strung plastic harp, about a foot high, that looked as if it might have come from the store's toy department. A black ribbon was tied to the harp.

"What the dickens is that?" said Bristol.

"Probably a gentle hint that I could be playing one of these very shortly." Angie tossed the harp on her office settee and walked back into her private office. At least her earlier caller hadn't gotten around to raiding her liquor cabinet. She took out a bottle of Beefeater gin.

"It's a trifle early," she told Jack Bristol, "but I think I could use a short snort." Gesturing toward the array of bottles: "Care to join me? You name it."

"Er, no thanks. I—I'm not really much of a drinker. Although I did have a few last night." He smiled nervously.

The fiery slug trickled down into Angie's tum, bearing its usual heart-warming message of hope and comfort.

"Speaking of last night, shall we pick up on your visit to Pike's hotel suite?" she prompted.

"I went there strictly on a wild hunch," said Jack.

"A hunch about what?"

"That Laidlaw Pike might know something about Dad's murder."

"What gave you that idea?"

"For one thing, they knew each other from way back. In fact, in a letter I got from Dad shortly before he was shot, he mentioned meeting Pike in a New York bar. Also and more important is what Pike's been doing since then."

"You mean oil prospecting in South America?"

"Not just South America. Colombia. And darn close to the territory where Emerald's been prospecting—in the Meta River country east of the cordilleras. To me that's not just a coincidence."

"You're suggesting—what?"

"Well . . . I'm not sure exactly. But look at it this way. Why would a shoestring operator like Pike gamble

60

on a prospect down in that area if an Emerald party had just brought back a negative report?"

Angie shrugged. "I pass. Why?"

"Maybe it's because Pike picked up some inside data or maps or whatever by crooked means—from some dishonest Emerald Oil employee. Dad found out what was going on, so he had to be silenced. With a bullet."

"Well, it's a theory," said Angie. "Did you find anything to support it?"

"Not really. I . . . To tell you the truth, I was so rattled I hardly knew what I was doing. I left Pike's suite about twenty minutes after you did."

Jack Bristol gulped and began to pace about the office. He stopped and looked at Angela Harpe. He was trying to keep his mind on business, trying to think of this attractive young Negro woman as an experienced private eye who could help him track down his father's killer. But it was damnably hard to shut out the memory of what had happened last night in Pike's hotel room—and the way she'd looked when he walked in on her this morning. That beautiful rear end turned toward him, bare breasts swinging distractingly as she whirled, gun in hand. Try as he might to discipline his thoughts, they kept focusing obsessively on the contents of Angela Harpe's skin-tight blue pantsuit.

Angie watched him, poker-faced, perfectly aware by the usual male-female telepathy of exactly what was going on in his head.

"Miss Harpe, will you help me?"

The Dark Angel dimpled. "Tell you what, Mr. Bristol. Why don't you take me to lunch and talk me into it?"

Jack Bristol smiled like the sun coming out and repressed a powerful urge to kiss her. They went down the street to a pleasantly dark and cavernous little pub called Nell Gwynn's Snug, where Angie ordered a gin

61

and tonic and Jack agreed to a Tom Collins to keep her company.

"Miss Harpe, I—I guess no gentleman would bring up what happened last night, but there's something I'd like to say—if you won't be offended."

Angie waved her hand. "Feel free, Mr. Bristol."

"Well, you see, I was brought up pretty strictly, and I guess you might say I've always lived a pretty strait-laced, humdrum sort of life—at least before I went to South America last winter. I even missed the draft. So when I decided to break into Laidlaw Pike's hotel suite, believe me, it took quite a bit of nerve. I even had to prime myself with a few drinks—which is quite against my usual principles."

Angie grinned. "I thought I detected a faint aroma of bourbon."

"When you came out of that bedroom, Miss Harpe, I just about went through the floor, I was so scared. And when you mentioned the bell captain, that spooked me even worse. I thought maybe you'd been dozing off there for a few hours, and I had visions of him coming up to check and tell you Pike was gone for the evening —that you'd missed him. Oh man, I was really flustered. I wanted you out of there but fast, before the roof fell in!"

Jack Bristol gave another nervous gulp and took a drink of his Tom Collins before going on. "The trouble was I—I'd never in my life seen anything so beautiful and disturbing as you, Miss Harpe. And you were offering to have sexual relations with me! You see, I wanted you to clear out in the worst way, but deep down I also couldn't help wanting you to stay even more, and . . . well, I was half drunk and hysterical, and I —I just wanted you to understand why I behaved like such a stupid jerk. All that loudmouth moralizing and whatnot. I—I just didn't want you to think I didn't appreciate what you were offering me last night. Or that I don't respect you, in spite of what happened."

Angie wanted to laugh, but he was speaking so seriously she stifled the urge. "Mr. Bristol, that's a very nice speech, and I do understand, and I never thought for a moment you didn't appreciate my little gift of sex—certainly not after the way you performed. I also think you're a very mell-mannered, nicely brought-up young man, and therefore there're a few things I should say to *you.*"

"Please do, Miss Harpe."

"Thank you, I shall. First, I suggest you call me Angie and I call you Jack. Second, since you're an alumnus of such a distinguished university as the California Institute of Technology, I'd like you to know that I'm what they call in the East a 'Cliffie'—which is to say, a Radcliffe girl. But I was brought up in Harlem and I've lived through some very seamy times and scenes, and I say 'shit' and 'fuck' and do both. I just want you to know all that at the outset, so we can be quite comfortable with each other, if I do decide to take your case."

Jack winced slightly at her language but said, "I'll bear all that in mind, Angie. And I certainly hope you *will* take the case and help find my father's killer."

Angie waited till her eggs benedict had been served before adding, "There's another little matter I probably ought to touch on, Jack. My fees aren't cheap, even when I'm working for a good-looking young dude like you. And of course I can't guarantee success."

Jack Bristol nodded. "I understand. Fergus Doyle and Wagner Axby of Emerald Oil have posted a ten thousand dollar reward for information leading to the arrest of my father's murderer. I have more than ten thousand of my own saved up. And Dad's life insurance policy established a hundred thousand dollar trust fund for me. Will that do for openers?"

"We're in business, baby. Which reminds me. Just how did you get into Pike's hotel room last night?"

"I saw him in the cloakroom at the Petroleum Society dinner and got a soap impression of the key in his coat pocket. Then I filed a blank to match. Bit hasty and amateurish, but it worked."

The Dark Angel smiled approvingly. "You know, Jack, I think you and I are going to get along just fine."

"May I, uh—ask what *you* were doing in Pike's hotel suite?"

Angie outlined her commission from Xerxes Zagrevi without going into details. "Speaking of Zagrevi, did you tell Doyle or Axby that you were coming to see me?"

"I told Fergus Doyle."

"Good. Then maybe I should start at the top by talking to him."

"Exactly what I was going to suggest, Angie."

"Where's his office?"

"He doesn't have one. Well, actually he does, I suppose, but he hardly uses it any more. You see, he's paralyzed from the waist down."

Angie gave a slight frown. "A wheelchair case?"

"Yeah, he was in a car accident a few years ago. Since then he's been spending most of his time at a country place upstate on Lake Nippigong."

"Doesn't that sort of cramp his style as board chairman?"

"It's pretty much an honorary post, anyhow," said Jack. "Wagner Axby's the real operating boss and chief executive officer. Besides, Doyle was one of the original founders of Emerald Oil, and he still owns a pretty good hunk of the stock. So he's not exactly the kind of guy they can give the old heave-ho to any time they feel like it."

Over coffee, Angie asked, "Where exactly is Lake Nippigong?"

"Roughly, up between the Catskills and the Adirondacks, if that gives you any idea. It's about a hundred and seventy-five miles from here, mostly up the New York State Thruway. If it's agreeable, I'd like to drive you."

"You have the transportation all planned?"

"No problem. As I told you, I'm in this group from Houston that was brought here to talk with Staroleum. We're getting the full Visiting Firemen treatment. Mrs. Kenning, who's head of Staroleum, has even provided us all with cars and unlimited gasoline from their own pumps."

"Ah, yes," said Angie, "the ever-lovely Star Kenning. She-wolf of Wall Street—and other points north, east, south and west."

"You know her?"

"I've run into her at a couple of cocktail parties. Of course she's, uh, also been in the gossip columns a good deal." Angie found herself wondering how that voracious pursuer of the *lingam* or male principle, commonly known as pecker, was making out with a handsome young innocent like Jack Bristol. Making out, no doubt.

Jack and Angie strolled from Nell Gwynn's back to *A. Harpe*'s office, where Jack made a phone call to Fergus Doyle at Lake Nippigong and was cordially told to come forthwith. "He's even invited us to spend the night," Jack reported, hanging up.

"That's very nice of him, but actually I had something else in mind," said Angie, and was gratified to see a flicker of disappointment dim Jack Bristol's eager-eyed look.

"Apparently Wagner Axby's with him," Jack added. "He came up this morning—although Mr. Doyle wasn't sure he'd still be there when we arrived."

"How nice. Maybe we can quiz them both for clues at the same time."

Angela Harpe and her new client took a cab from

65

42nd Street to the parking garage on East 50th near Lexington, where Jack Bristol's courtesy car was stabled, a block from the Warrick Plaza.

A man was lounging in a steel-tubing chair inside the glassed-in cubicle near the garage door, chewing a cold cigar and idly scanning a rumpled copy of the *Daily News*. He dropped the paper and came sauntering out —a big man in an expensive suit and hand-made shoes, with hard eyes and vein-mottled cheeks. He moved with the arrogant swagger of a person used to throwing his weight around and seeing apprehensive, placating looks appear on the faces of people he spoke to.

"You Jack Bristol?"

"That's right."

"And this little dinge is the Dark Angel, huh?" The big man grinned coldly and undressed Angie with his eyes, assessing her price as a piece of ass.

"What do you want?" said Jack curtly.

The big man gave Bristol a slow, insolent stare, chewing his cigar and putting Jack in *his* place. "Mr. Axby," he announced, "doesn't want you slumming around with this broad. I'm taking over the investigation of your father's murder."

Jack's brows puckered in a startled frown. "What are you, a private detective?"

"No, he's a New York City cop—Lieutenant Coogin, NYPD," said Angie, who made it her business to know such things. "Apparently on the pad, since he's taking orders from a private businessman."

The big cop's eyes blazed. "Let's see your license, chippy."

"Let's see your ID, fatass."

He stepped closer, his face and manner menacing. "You want your meal ticket lifted?"

Angie gave him a bored smile. "You and your boss

66

can take that up with the Columbia Insurance Underwriters and the Trans-National Bankers Association. If you think you've got enough clout."

A Pontiac Firebird had just come rolling off the elevator. The Puerto Rican attendant got out, his eyes glued to the developing scene in obvious fascination.

"Wait a minute," Jack Bristol said to Coogin. "What's this all about?"

Coogin shouldered him roughly aside. "You keep out of this, Bud. Looks like I may have to bust some ass around here." To Angie: "Get moving, nigger. Or do I have to toss you in the tank with the rest of the Times Square whores?"

"Kiss my black American butt—you cornholing Mick bogtrotter."

Coogin's eyes flared with sadistic rage. His big ham hand doubled into a fist crashing toward Angie's jaw. But the blow never landed, for reasons difficult to determine due to the speed of what followed.

Next thing Jack Bristol knew, the hulking plainclothesman went hurtling past her into a cement column. The impact crumpled Coogin to the floor. He raised himself slowly upright, shaking off the daze, his face murderous. One hand came out from inside his coat, clutching a big Colt .44. Angie kicked him in the teeth and his manner became more docile, if somewhat lethargic.

She retrieved the gun, broke open the cylinder and emptied out the magnum cartridges before dropping the piece at Coogin's feet.

"Can you hear me, Coogin? My lawyers, who happen to be Lynchthorpe, Greenbaum & Foley of 7 Wall Street, will have a full report on the commissioner's desk before the end of the day if you don't get your fat ass out of here pronto. You dig?" Turning to Jack Bristol, she added pleasantly, "Shall we go?"

The Puerto Rican attendant brushed aside Jack's proffered tip. He hastily opened the Firebird's door for Angie and murmured with an adoring glance, "Right on, Mama!"

Chapter Seven

"I take it," said Angie as the Firebird rolled north along the East River, "that the 'well-known oil executive' who helped you locate me was *not* Wagner Axby."

"Too right," said Jack, looking embarrassed. "It was Fergus Doyle. Since he's the one I know best, he was naturally the one I turned to."

With a glance at the lovely black girl seated beside him, Jack added, "I'm sorry about what happened back there, Angie."

"Don't give it a thought. Private eyes aren't the world's most popular personalities—especially the black female type. Just off the top of your head, though, have you any idea why Axby might be sensitive to your hiring an outside investigator?"

Jack gave a baffled shrug. "Only the obvious one—that he doesn't want any outsider nosing around or stirring things up while these negotiations are underway with Staroleum."

The Dark Angel mused, "Could be, I suppose. Although it does tend to raise the question—what's he got to hide?"

"Darned if I know. But if Axby does have anything to hide, I hope you'll find it."

"One can only try. Never know what'll turn up under the next rock."

They cruised through the Bronx and Westchester and crossed the Hudson over the Tappan Zee Bridge. Only later, as they were skirting Bear Mountain, did Angie lead the conversation back toward the case at hand.

"What about this dude we're going to see—Fergus Doyle?"

"What about him?"

"Give me a little background."

"Mm, well, he's around seventy, I'd say. Nice-looking old guy, white-haired, very dignified and upright in spite of his wheelchair. Used to be a hard-driving disciplinarian from all I hear. He seems more mellow now, though."

"He lives alone?" asked Angie.

"With a servant couple. Actually he did have a wife and a foster son, but they're both dead."

"What happened?"

"The boy was a nephew they'd adopted—his sister's son. Got on drugs in the 1960s and died of an OD. I guess they were both very fond of him. Then his wife died of cancer soon afterward. Apparently Doyle's never really gotten over that double loss. The accident that crippled him was the final straw."

"Yet he's still active in the company—at least he's board chairman."

Jack Bristol said, "Well, as I told you, he was one of the founders—a real gung-ho empire-builder type, from what they say. No doubt chairing the board still gives him some sense of identity—something to cling to. But I think he's mostly going through the motions now. I don't think he cares all that much *what* happens to Emerald Oil any more."

Late in the afternoon Jack stopped the Firebird on a wooded road, in front of a wide rustic wooden gate. The gate bore a sign saying:

LAKE NIPPIGONG
BIRD & WILDLIFE SANCTUARY

Private Property
Emerald Oil Co.

Open to Visitors 10:00 AM to 6:00 PM
Saturdays & Sundays

HUNTING OR FISHING
STRICTLY PROHIBITED!

Jack got out of the car to open the gate, then drove
through and closed it again behind them.

"What's this sanctuary bit?" asked Angie as they
drove on.

"Probably the main interest in Doyle's life right now,"
Jack said. "He's always been a nature lover, I guess. He
started spreading food for the migratory birds, and now
flocks of them come back every season, spring and fall
—in fact, some stay here all year round. I think he has
hopes of turning the place into a public preserve eventually."

The road wound on and on through open fields and
groves of scented greenery—oak, ash, maple, beech,
birch, pine, rhododendron, mountain laurel. Angie spotted a dozen or more of the commoner birds that she
could recognize—like jays, finches, cardinals, doves,
woodpeckers, flickers, bobwhites—and from the shore
of the lake in the distance an occasional heron or other
waterfowl rose flapping into view.

"How big is the spread?" she asked.

"Oh, several thousand acres, I should think. It completely encloses the lake. Actually it's company land, but
him being board chairman and all, they've allowed him
to live on it and develop it as a nature sanctuary."

Through a screen of trees, a pleasant-looking house of weathered gray fieldstone came distantly into view.

"Which reminds me," said Jack. "I should probably warn you about Doyle's servant."

"What's to warn?"

"His appearance. It may come as a shock if you're not prepared for it. He's a regular giant. Stands around six-six or six-seven, and he must weigh at least three hundred pounds."

"I've seen big men before," smiled Angela Harpe.

"Not with a head like his, believe me. This guy's an ex-coal miner from Pennsylvania—Polish, I think. Mr. Doyle just calls him Nemo. He was hurt in a mine cave-in or rock slide or something—so badly it took a plastic surgeon to put him back together. Only I guess the coal company wouldn't spring for any top-drawer medical talent. The poor guy ended up looking like something out of a horror movie. His vocal cords were hurt, too, so he even talks funny."

They were approaching the house at an angle from the rear. As the Firebird swept around the curve of the graveled entrance drive, they saw a majestic dark green Mercedes-Benz and several figures at the porticoed front entrance.

Jack Bristol slowed with a feeling of resentful embarrassment. Damn! He had purposely dawdled all the way from town to avoid seeing Wagner Axby. And now they'd arrived just in time to meet him face to face as he was leaving.

Angie saw him, too—and typed him at a glance. The kind of thick-necked, red-faced, arrogant bullshitter who showed up on TV as an "oil industry spokesman" at the height of the fuel crisis. To warn the great mouth-breathing American public that it had damned well better rejoice at his company's 97 percent increase in profits and go on gratefully coughing up extortionate tax subsidies, or he might just decide to squeeze off their gasoline trickle altogether.

Apparently Axby had just finished saying goodbye to Fergus Doyle, who was in his wheelchair outside the front door of the house. And now as Axby turned toward his limousine, his eyes fell on the Firebird and its two occupants. His face darkened.

Jack Bristol and Angie got out of the car.

"Didn't my man contact you?" Axby growled at Jack.

"Your man?"

"The detective. Coogin."

"Oh. Yes, sir. We saw him at the garage just before we left the city."

"I've assigned him to take over the investigation of your father's murder. Didn't he tell you? I want this"—Axby gestured toward the Dark Angel with a contemptuous jerk of his head, otherwise pointedly ignoring her presence—"*person* off the case."

"Sorry, Mr. Axby," said Jack Bristol evenly, "but Coogin's changed his mind. He's decided to withdraw from the case."

"Withdraw?" Axby scowled intimidatingly. "What the hell is that supposed to mean?"

Angela Harpe suddenly lost patience. "It means we left him flat on his ass, meathead. He didn't come on too well as Sam Spade. So he decided he'd better stop running errands for would-be bigshots like you and go back to earning his pension as a city cop. Otherwise he might find himself facing charges."

Axby's face had taken on a mulberry tinge. "Look, you black slut," he said in his toughest oilfield-roughneck voice. "I haven't been in this business for thirty years without learning how to deal with chiseling harpies like you. So I'm warning you right now, sister, in terms even you can dig. You stick your nigger nose in Emer-

73

ald Oil's affairs, and they'll be fishing your ass out of the Harlem River. Understand?"

"Are you threatening me, Mr. Axby?" said Angie sweetly.

Perhaps her tone of voice and her use of "Mister" tempted Axby into believing he'd gotten through. His square red face cracked in a hard, cold smile. "Just laying it on the line, baby, so you'll know exactly where I'm coming from."

"Good." Angie slid her shoulder bag down into her hands. "I just wanted to get that straight because, you see, the clasp of this bag contains a little microphone pickup wired to a miniature tape recorder inside. And now that I have your voice and Lt. Coogin's voice on tape, I think my attorneys will have all they need to bring grand jury charges of conspiracy and attempted coercion."

Axby's surge of rage was palpable and deadly as heat lightning triggering a thunderclap. He advanced toward the Dark Angel, both hands working. "Why, you goddamned little—"

He got no farther because just then Angie swung her bag smartly between his legs. The impact of the steel-bar-weighted frame was even more discouraging than a knee in the balls. Axby staggered back against the Mercedes, clutching his crotch with both hands. His red face had gone sickly pale and he looked as if he might vomit.

Axby's husky uniformed chauffeur, who had been standing near the door of the limousine, moved to his boss's rescue—and found himself facing a Baby Browning.

"Get Bigmouth in the car and split," the Dark Angel ordered curtly. "If I have to look at that ugly fucking face of his much longer, I may lose my temper."

The chauffeur obeyed.

74

There was dead silence as the Mercedes drove off.

Angie turned to the old man in the wheelchair—and noticed with a start that a huge figure was now standing beside it. "I apologize, Mr. Doyle," she said in a gently melodious contralto. "It was unforgivable, becoming involved in such a scene with your guest. I shouldn't have let him get under my skin. If you'd rather I leave, perhaps Jack will be good enough to drive me to the nearest bus station. Or I suppose I can always thumb a ride."

"I'm sure you can, my dear, with no difficulty at all, being as beautiful as you are." The old man's leathery face bore a smile of genuine friendliness and admiration. "But please don't even consider it. Axby brought what happened on himself—he left you no choice. He was always a bullying, overbearing fool. A good man, you understand—excellent at getting things done—but a little too impressed with his own importance. . . . Jack, my boy, how are you!" The matter was dismissed as of no further interest.

"Fine, thank you, sir." Bristol moved forward to shake hands. "I appreciate your attitude, and I'm glad you approve of Miss Harpe as much as I do. Actually, she was only doing what *I* should have done on her behalf—but she seems to know how to take care of herself a lot better than I could."

"Indeed she does," chuckled Doyle. "By the way—it's *Angela* Harpe, I believe?"

"Call me Angie."

"Thank you, my dear." He took her hand. "And I hope you'll pay me the compliment of calling me Fergus, as I've already invited Jack to do. But dear me, what are we lingering out here for? Do come in and let's all have a drink!"

Doyle's huge manservant opened the door and stood aside to let them enter. Angie's glance brushed him in passing. Jesus, what a Frankenstein monster! No wonder Jack had tried to prepare her for a shock. . . .

Actually, she'd heard of a similar case before, from a black vet who'd served in the Persian Gulf Command during World War II. The case of an Iranian dockside laborer who'd gotten his head crushed between two crates while a Victory ship was being offloaded—apparently with no permanent ill effect, other than a visibly lopsided skull.

In the case of Doyle's manservant, Nemo, his skull wasn't lopsided, it was—well, compacted. The result seemed to be no neck and very little forehead. His scalp must have been torn loose, Angie decided, and when it was sewn back, his hairline had been brought damn near down to his eyebrows, making him look a trifle like the comic-strip caveman, Alley Oop. Except that the bony structure of Nemo's eye sockets, or orbits, had somehow been squeezed forward under the impact of the rock-fall accident, giving his eyeballs a permanent froglike bulge.

"What'll it be?" Fergus was asking. "Nemo here can mix almost anything."

"What are you having?" said Angie.

"Bourbon and branch water, my dear. My regular tipple."

"That'll do me fine."

"Make it three," Jack concurred.

They were in a long, narrow parlor or sitting room that seemed to run the entire length of the house. The furnishings were neither new nor fashionable, but the overall effect was extraordinarily charming.

A dramatic sweep of window looked out on the tree-fringed lake, alive with waterfowl. The walls were pine-paneled, and the Shiraz carpeting underfoot was well-worn but still glowingly beautiful. Among the jumble of comfortable hassocks and chairs, leather and chintz-covered, was the most beautiful Morris chair An-

76

gie had ever seen, obviously Doyle's own favorite. The rugged stone fireplace was flanked by well-stocked bookcases, their shelves lined with books that had obviously been read, many of them more than once.

"What a lovely place!" said Angie.

Fergus Doyle warmed to the patent sincerity in her voice. "Your good taste confirms my high opinion of you, my dear," he chuckled.

"How long have you had it?"

"Well, the house was built back in the early 1950s by the former owner of this lake property. Then after Emerald Oil acquired it, we began coming here during the summers, when my wife and our—our foster son were still alive. I moved in for what I thought would be six months or so, to convalesce after my accident. But I found I couldn't leave."

Doyle chuckled again and waved his arm. "What kind of a fool would I be to go back to the city from all this! The telephone puts me in as close touch with our key personnel as if I were back at my office in Rockefeller Center. When the occasion demands, I'm only three hours from Manhattan by car, hardly an hour by helicopter."

Jack and Angie murmured polite agreement.

"You seem to have done a remarkable job in developing the lake as a bird sanctuary," the Dark Angel added.

"Thank you, Angie. Yes, I've tried to do my bit for nature." Doyle's face softened to a look of brooding peace as his gaze panned out the window. "I sometimes think it's the one worthwhile thing I've accomplished in my life. Not that it was all that difficult—the lake lies directly on what's called the Atlantic Flyway, which is the regular migratory route for birds between Eastern Canada and points south."

As Nemo silently served the drinks, Doyle went on,

"I must take you both out on the lake and introduce you to some of our feathered guests while you're here."

"I'd enjoy that," said Angie. She sipped her bourbon. "But I'd better not beat around the bush, Fergus. You know why I've come. Am I to understand that, unlike Wagner Axby, you do *not* disapprove of my investigation?"

"Certainly not," said Doyle. "I think it's an excellent idea, getting a professional sleuth like yourself on the case. Jack's father was one of my oldest and closest friends—and the police have done little or nothing to solve his murder."

"I'm not sure I can do much better. He was killed eight months ago and the trail may be totally cold by now." Angie took another warming slug of her drink. "Jack thinks his father's murder had something to do with the oil business. What's your opinion, Fergus?"

"I think he's right. Undoubtedly."

"Why?"

Doyle studied the amber contents of his glass. "Maybe I can explain it this way, Angie. Oil isn't called black gold for nothing. It's exactly like gold in the effect it has on some men—the way it utterly dominates their lives. Crazy as it may sound, they come to lust for petroleum the way a miser lusts for wealth. To them, the search for sources, the gamble of drilling, the thrill of bringing in a successful new well—all that becomes an obsession, quite aside from any question of personal enrichment— the same way an old desert-rat prospector goes on endlessly searching for gold, even though he knows in his heart of hearts he'll never wind up a penny richer."

"And Jack's father was like that?"

Doyle nodded. "I would say so." He shot a glance at Jack. "I'm sure you know how much affection I had for your dad. Will you be offended if I speak bluntly?"

"Of course not."

"Lang Bristol was what Graham Greene would probably call 'a burnt-out case.' No woman ever meant more than a passing roll in the hay to him after he and your mother separated. And he didn't give a damn for money. The one constant passion in his life was oil. The only times he ever came fully and completely alive were on prospecting expeditions in the field. Then he was like a bloodhound on the scent. That's why it's inconceivable to me that Lang could have been murdered for any other motive than oil."

"I see," Angie said thoughtfully. "If that's so, then Jack's theory about the timing seems even more persuasive."

"Timing?" Fergus Doyle frowned. "I'm not sure I follow."

"As I get the picture, Lang Bristol had just come back from a prospecting trip to South America which was officially labeled a failure. Yet immediately afterward rumors began to spread that Emerald Oil had made a strike. And at that interesting junction, Lang Bristol is found murdered. Do you consider that a mere coincidence?"

"Definitely not. I'm sure those circumstances helped trigger his killing."

Doyle finished his bourbon and set down his glass.

Angie watched him curiously. "Maybe we'd better go back to square one," she said. "You assured Jack that the official report calling the expedition a failure was correct. Is that the truth?"

"Yes, it's the truth." Fergus Doyle sighed softly before adding:

"But it's not the *whole* truth."

Chapter Eight

"Would you care to explain that last remark?" the Dark Angel said to Fergus Doyle.

"I'll try. But you must bear with me, my dear, if I seem to ramble. Oil hunting's come a long way since I was a youngster in the game—and even more so from the days when old John Carll tramped around, assembling data on the early wells. Today we know all about anticlines and slipped faults and stratigraphic traps and salt domes. We have gravimeters and magnetometers and all sorts of paraphernalia to help us. Yet when all's said and done, finding oil is still as much an art as it is a science. Many a good petroleum geologist or geophysicist still relies on his own hunches as much as he does on instrument readings."

"Did that apply to Dad?" put in Jack Bristol.

"Indeed it did. Lang had a nose for oil—that's the only way I can put it. More than once he's pointed our company drills dead on an oil pocket—without being able to explain in any rational way how he knew it was there."

"And did he have any hunches about this area you've been prospecting down in Colombia?" asked Angie.

"That's exactly what he had, my dear. When our first expedition returned last year, the data was all completely negative. Just as I told you, Jack. There was nothing —absolutely *nothing* on paper—to suggest we might be getting close to oil."

"But Lang Bristol thought differently?"

"He did. And I can tell you, Angie, it put us in a real bind. I'll be giving away no great secret if I tell you Emerald Oil was not in particularly healthy shape at that time. Many of our wells were running dry. We held no promising new leases. For myself, I was old and tired— I would just as soon have closed the books on Emerald Oil and sold off our assets for whatever they might bring."

Angie said, "Did Wagner Axby share that view?"

"No, of course not. He's a younger man, with his career still to think of. On the other hand, he's a much harder-nosed money man than I am—and less of a gambler. I came up in this business as a wildcatter. Wagner came up as an accountant—a man who could perform magic with a balance sheet."

"So what did you decide?" asked Jack.

"All things considered, we decided we'd have to write off that first expedition as a failure. And risk no more company money on exploration in that area of Colombia—regardless of whether or not your dad sniffed oil."

Angela Harpe frowned. "Then the rumors of a strike must have been based just on Lang Bristol's *hunch.*"

The old man nodded. "I agree, Angie—it's the only possible answer. Lang Bristol was a hard drinker—he may have talked in his cups, may have said things which were soon inflated by rumor into reports of a major oil strike."

"Which brings us to his murder."

"Ah, yes—a dark and tragic turn of events."

81

"All right, let's say Dad did talk out of turn," Jack mused grimly. "Why would a mere hunch incite anyone to murder him?"

"Perhaps," said Doyle, "the killer *agreed* with your father. Perhaps he had reasons of his own to believe there was oil in that part of Colombia—perhaps he even *knew*. And if your father kept on talking, there was danger he might arouse other prospectors' interest in the area. So he had to be silenced."

"Or maybe the killer *didn't* know beforehand," said Jack, suddenly pursuing a theory of his own. "But Dad convinced him. He might even have offered Dad a share of the venture to lead the prospecting team. And when Dad refused out of loyalty to Emerald Oil, he had to be silenced—as you say, to stop him from arousing any other prospector's interest in the area."

"Entirely possible."

"Or maybe," said Angie, "Lang Bristol had to be silenced for fear he might revive *Emerald Oil's* interest in the area."

"Shrewdly put, my dear Angie," said Fergus Doyle.

"And, in fact, that's more or less what happened?"

Again the old man nodded. "Correct. By the time Lang was killed, we'd already begun to have second thoughts about giving up in Colombia. And his murder . . . well, let's say it confirmed our feeling. Both Axby and I figured someone else must have inside data on that area—that he or they had killed Lang Bristol to protect their stake—and we'd damned well better take the plunge and play Lang's hunch or we might lose out on a major oil strike. So we gambled most of our available resources on a second prospect in Colombia."

"Has your gamble paid off?" the Dark Angel asked bluntly.

The old man in the wheelchair regarded her silently for a few moments. Then he smiled. "How to answer you, my dear? As an officer of Emerald Oil, I've no right to give away what's still a tightly held company secret. Yet I'm perfectly willing to trust your discretion and Jack's. Maybe the best way to answer is this. We're now negotiating with the investment banking house of Fox Wineburg to finance a new Emerald Oil stock issue in order to raise operating capital. Any knowledgeable Wall Streeter can tell you that—so Wagner Axby can hardly accuse me of leaking secret information. Feel free to draw your own conclusions."

Angela Harpe downed her own bourbon and smiled back at him. "I'm only a Wall Street amateur, Fergus—but one would hardly expect Emerald Oil to be raising operating capital if it didn't expect to do some extensive drilling."

Doyle went on smiling. "As I say, Angie—feel free to draw your own conclusions." He gestured suddenly toward the window. "But I think we've talked enough for now. Let me show you some of our lake dwellers before dinner."

A broad sweep of comfortably ragged lawn led down to the marshy, willow-curtained shore of the lake. Jack gently propelled the old man's wheelchair, although it was equipped with an electric motor. The wooden planks sounded underfoot as they went out on a long dock that extended over the reed-choked marsh into the lake. The western sky was red, and the air was clamorous with the cries of the waterfowl.

"Do you know much about birds, Angie?" said Fergus Doyle.

"Not a great deal. They weren't too prominent a feature of the scenery where I grew up, north of 110th Street."

"It's a great temptation to bore you with my nature lore, as I've bored Jack here in the past." As he spoke, a bird rose erect, flapping its wings, and went skittering past the dock as if it were walking on water. "Can you identify that one?" said Doyle with a grin.

"Coot, isn't it?" guessed Angie.

"Gallinule, but you're very close. The difference is mainly in bill color. Coots' beaks are chalky white instead of red."

Angie took out her Kensui binoculars. The Canada geese and several swans were obvious, but she was also able to pick out by name wood ducks, black ducks, mallards and mergansers.

"My dear, you're doing excellently," the old man applauded. "You're really the most knowledgeable guest I've had in a blue moon."

As dusk descended, an armada of larger, long-legged waterfowl began rising out of the marshes with a great beating of wings to soar gracefully over the lake. Doyle proudly pointed out great blue heron, American and snowy egrets and glossy ibis—the latter dark, dramatic-looking birds with long, down-curving bills, which sailed past with necks and wings outstretched.

"This is our prime spectacle of the day," he commented. "They feed in the marshes on fish and frogs all during the daylight hours, and then at twilight return to their nests."

"Down at the other end of the lake?" asked Angie.

"Yes, their rookery's on a big sandspit. We have them here all summer, you know. We're even getting wood storks now. Up until recently, they'd only been spotted in New York once during the whole past century."

The old man talked of hawks and ospreys and bald eagles and peregrine falcons. It was obvious he'd become a genuine ornithological expert, and his enthusiasm was infectious. But at last, when a huge dark figure sounded a dinner bell from the lighted doorway, Doyle led them back to the house.

The meal of Beef Wellington was delicious, presumably cooked by Mrs. Nemo, who glided darkly and silently into view from time to time to help her husband with the serving. Angie filed her as a probable Mohawk Indian, middle-aged but still astonishingly beautiful to have mated with such a grotesque giant.

After finishing their apple pie, they moved to comfortable lounge chairs to enjoy their Irish coffee.

Jack Bristol said, "May I ask you something, Fergus?"

"Of course, my boy. Fire away."

"From what you told Angie and me this afternoon, it seems you think Dad was shot by an outsider—maybe a wildcatter or someone from another oil company. In fact that's what persuaded you to send another team down to Colombia."

"True."

"Yet when I first came here and got to know you after Dad's funeral, you allowed me to believe his murderer might be someone inside Emerald Oil itself. That's why I got you to send me along on this last prospecting expedition."

Doyle nodded. "Quite so. I plead guilty, Jack. But don't think for a moment I discount that theory entirely, even now. I still think we may have an enemy within—if not the killer himself, then someone who's working with him. It may have been a tip from an insider that led the murderer to seek out your father in the first place—and prime him with liquor to get him talking. Even now, with your father out of the way, he may still want an inside ally—to keep him informed of Emerald Oil's moves and leases."

Jack frowned thoughtfully. "Mm, I see what you mean, sir."

Angie got up to indulge in one of her pet pastimes—looking over the titles in other people's bookcases. Apparently Doyle was a reader of catholic tastes, ranging all the way from Smollett's translation of *Gil Blas* through poetry, biography and history to Ian Fleming's *Thunderball*. But the shelves were also heavily interlarded with bird books, like *Waterfowl Tomorrow,* and scholarly tomes on the oil industry.

Angie was curious enough to glance through several of the latter. From between the pages of *Enterprise in Oil* by Kendall Beaton, a snapshot fell out.

She stooped to pick it up—and felt a sudden electrifying thrill of interest. The snapshot showed two men chatting in deck chairs, each with a drink in his hand, apparently on shipboard. One, in khaki bush shirt and shorts, was a lean, rugged, balding, deeply tanned outdoorsy type somewhere in his late fifties. The other, in blazer and white ducks, was old, vulturine and unmistakable. Angie had seen his face on the cover of *Time* magazine only weeks before. And seen him masked but in the flesh only last night. It was Xerxes Zagrevi.

Jack saw her change of expression. "Find something?" He strolled over to join her, and the next moment his own face changed. "Hey, that's Dad!"

The Dark Angel turned to Doyle. "When was this taken?" She brought the snapshot over to show him.

Doyle stared at it, obviously puzzled. "Hanged if I know. . . . You found it in the bookcase?"

"Yes, in the pages of one of the books—as if someone had been using it as a bookmark."

The old man shook his head slowly. "I'm sure this will sound ridiculous, but I don't ever recall seeing it before."

"Can either of you *estimate* when it was taken? . . . just from Mr. Bristol's appearance?"

"Within the last couple of years, I'd say," replied Doyle. "Wouldn't you, Jack?"

"Yes, I suppose so—although you saw more of Dad than I did."

"Judging from this, Lang Bristol and Xerxes Zagrevi must have been acquainted. . . ." Angie's words were half statement, half question.

Doyle nodded. "Probably. Lang was well known throughout the industry. And of course Zagrevi's a public figure."

"When might they have met?"

The old man shrugged. "Zagrevi's yacht, *Rudabah,* was down in the Caribbean last year. I suppose they might have met at Baranquilla."

The Dark Angel studied the photo thoughtfully. "Mind if I keep this, Fergus?"

"Of course not, my dear. Please do, if you think it may help in any way."

Jack and Angie left soon afterward. As they drove back along the winding road to the highway, a 'possum came scuttling out of the brush—then froze in the glare of the Firebird's headlights, rolled over and lay still.

Jack waited until he had replaced the entrance gate and they were heading East toward the Thruway before asking, "Well, did you learn anything?"

"Quite a bit. Whether it puts us any closer to your father's killer is something else again."

"What about that snapshot?"

"Well . . . let's say it's interesting."

"Think it means anything?"

"Good question. If it *was* taken last summer, presumably Zagrevi might have learned then about your father's hunch—but if he did, it's funny he hasn't followed up and had the area prospected for E-Z Oil."

Jack nodded, frowning. "I agree. Besides, Dad wouldn't have lasted in this business if he'd been all that irresponsible. I mean, he may have talked too much when he got tanked up—but in a case like this, I think he'd keep a tight rein on his tongue—at least until the expedition was over and all the reports were in."

"You mean until he'd reported to Doyle and Axby, and they had decided not to play his hunch?"

"Right. Once that happened, he probably figured it didn't matter any more to Emerald Oil if he did blab. And remember—it wasn't until that time that rumors of a big strike began to spread."

There was a brief silence. "How fast can we make it back to New York, Jack?"

"Oh, maybe by eleven, if I step on it."

"Step on it."

The Firebird zoomed through the darkness. "You, uh, have a late date tonight?"

"I'm thinking of paying a return visit to Laidlaw Pike's hotel suite," said Angie.

Jack Bristol was suddenly very conscious of the female figure beside him as the memory of last night's frenetic copulation flashed through his mind. It was almost as if he could feel the Dark Angel's sexual radiations. "Think you might turn up some evidence?" he asked, trying to keep his voice casual.

"When I searched his rooms last night, I wasn't looking for evidence that might link him to an insider at Emerald Oil," Angie explained. "Also, if he does have a map or any other secret to hide, there's *one* place I failed to look."

It was almost a quarter past eleven as they drove through the echoing streets of midtown Manhattan. Angie had Jack stop at a curbside phone booth while she called the Hotel Thermidor and asked for Pike's room number. After ringing a while, the operator said, "I'm sorry, there's no answer."

"Could you give me the desk, please?" To the clerk, Angie said, "I've been trying to reach Mr. Pike in 715, but he doesn't answer. It's rather urgent. Do you have any idea where he's gone or when he might come back?"

"No—o—o . . . but let me see. I was on the desk when Mr. Pike went out. That was around nine o'clock as I recall. I believe he said something about going to Long Island."

"Then I suppose he's apt to be late getting back."

"I would think so, yes."

"If I leave a message, could you make sure it reaches him when he comes in?"

"Yes, of course. I'll be on duty till two."

Angie named a bar a block or so from the Thermidor. "If he gets back before midnight or 12:30, would you please ask him to come and look for me there? I may not be able to stay put, so if I'm not around when he first comes in, ask him please to wait at the bar for a while. And sign the message 'Miss Nightgrove for X.Z.' "

"Miss Nightgrove for X.Z.?" The clerk' stone invited further explanation.

"He'll know what it means." Angie hung up and got back in the car with Jack Bristol. "Okay, the coast should be clear for a while."

"Can I come up with you?"

"Well—sure, if you want to. Might be safer if you stayed down in the lobby, so you could warn me if Pike shows up. On the other hand, I suppose two heads may be better than one when it comes to searching. But we'll have to be damned careful going in the lobby together at this hour. Bell captains and desk clerks have such nasty minds."

Again, to avoid the doorman, the Dark Angel made a cautious entry by the hotel's side door. As it turned out, the lobby was semi-dark and quiet as a tomb, except for a couple in evening dress chatting on one of the sofas. The desk clerk was busily absorbed in checking through guest cards and making entries in a ledger. Neither the bell captain nor any bellhop was in sight.

She beckoned to Jack. They crossed the lobby briskly and went up in the elevator. Outside the door of 715, she asked softly, "Still got that key you made?"

"Right here." He inserted it and, after a bit of manipulation, got the door open.

Somewhat unnervingly, all the lights were on. But a search quickly proved the suite was empty.

"Pike must've left them on to scare off burglars," guessed Angie. "Maybe one of us left traces of our visit last night."

"Probably me," said Jack Bristol. "I was so darned rattled, I could've left clues scattered all over the suite."

"Well, let's take a look at that secret hiding place I mentioned. Then we'll tackle the desk."

Angie led the way into the bedroom. While she was picking the trunk lock, she said, "Don't jump when you see what's in here. It's only a dummy."

Nevertheless, Bristol gave a slight strangled gasp at sight of the redhead. "Holy cats. She looks awfully real. You sure that's just a—a dummy?"

"Positive." Angie pulled the figure out of the trunk and, with Jack's help, laid it on the bed.

"What the heck is it for?"

"Three guesses."

Jack Bristol gave her an innocently wide-eyed stare. "You mean . . . for . . . for simulated sexual purposes?"

Angie grinned and nodded. "It's a sex robot. And not all that unusual, either—though, of course, the general public never reads about them. I'm told they originated in postwar Japan, but now they're made in half a dozen countries. Including this one."

"B–B–But I mean—who the dickens would want one?"

"Dirty old men mostly. Or rather *rich* dirty old men. Maybe rich dirty young ones, for that matter. This thing probably cost at least ten Gs. I suppose it's one way to avoid VD."

As she spoke, she was peeling off the doll's panties. Its mound was furred with red pubic hair. "Well, well," murmured Angie. "How very realistic."

She inspected the doll's body carefully, including both armpits, and eventually found what she was looking for at the nape of the neck, hidden under its hair—a slotted electrical socket for recharging and a small switch button. Angie pressed the button.

Almost at once she could feel the plastic flesh begin to warm beneath her fingers. A subtle funky aroma of female perspiration and genital exudation rose to her nostrils. The dummy's hips began to move in a suggestive rhythm. Its arms reached out, its eyes opened and closed, its lips moved.

"Oh, please! . . . Fuck me, darling! . . . Fuck me hard!"

As the recorded voice spoke from somewhere inside the robot's head, its knees moved up and back, its hips revolved upward, and its thighs spread wide, revealing the moistly open lips of incredibly realistic genitals.

"Sorry, sister," giggled Angie. "I've got a headache tonight."

She inserted her fingers into the doll's vagina. When she withdrew them a moment later, she brought out three dark-green, glassy-looking pebbles, ranging in size from a peanut to an almond.

"For Pete's sake," muttered Jack Bristol, who had watched the whole operation incredulously. "What are those things?"

"They're not kidney stones, lover," said Angie. "Off the top of my head, I'd say they're raw emeralds."

Chapter Nine

"Raw emeralds?" echoed Jack Bristol.

"Stones that haven't been cut or polished yet."

"Yeah, sure, I know that. But I mean—why the dickens is he hiding valuable gemstones in—in a place like this?"

"You know how easily hotel rooms get broken into these days."

Jack took one of the stones and held it up to the light. Even unfaceted and unpolished, he could sense its deep glowing green fire. "What're you going to do with 'em, Angie?"

The Dark Angel shrugged. "Put them back, what else. I'm not sure what good the information does us, but at least now we know what Pike's hiding up his sleeve. Or up his dolly's twat, to be precise."

She inserted the emeralds, one by one, back into the robot's vagina, then switched off its electrical mechanism. As its limbs stopped working obscenely, the recorded voice spoke again from inside its head—this time with a slight "dying fall" Doppler effect as the mechanism ran down:

"Oh gee, that was wonderful, baby! . . . You're a terrific fucker!"

"Thanks, kid—you're not bad yourself," said Angie. "At Disney World, you'd make a million."

She glanced at her wristwatch as she pulled on the doll's panties. "Come on, we'd better work fast. Let's get this thing back in the trunk and go see what we can find in Pike's desk."

To speed the search, Angie took the drawers on one side of the desk, Jack the other side.

"Remember, we're looking for anything that may link Pike to your father—or any other source of inside information at Emerald Oil."

The drawers were cluttered with bank statements; bills, paid and unpaid; direct mail ads and solicitations; personal letters; outdated insurance policies; jotted memoranda; clippings; documents of various kinds—the paper debris of a decade or more. Pike's passbooks and checkbooks totaled only about eight or nine thousand in cash on hand, and apparently he had no stock holdings or other investments, unless these were on deposit in some bank vault.

Curiously, Angie noticed, there was little or no material relating to his recent oil-prospecting expedition.

"Wait a minute," she said suddenly. "Remember what you were telling me about the field data from your expedition being sent back to Houston for evaluation? I mean, like the seismograph records and all that?"

Jack Bristol said, "Yeah. A pickup truck took our daily reports from camp to the nearest post office every morning."

"So what about the data from Pike's expedition?"

Jack frowned a moment. "He must have an office somewhere."

"Where? Not in New York or Houston—at least not from what Zagrevi was telling me last night."

"Well . . . maybe he evaluated all the data on a day-to-day basis."

"Surely he'd keep *some* kind of records," Angie pointed out. "I don't know much about the oil business, but wouldn't he need some pretty exact information to refer to, when it came to leasing land? He could hardly keep all that data in his memory."

"No, that's true," muttered Jack, looking puzzled.

"For that matter, what about all the bookkeeping?— the pay records and expense accounts, the government forms, all the financial and legal red tape involved in staging the expedition?"

"It's not here, that's for sure. But don't ask me where he's got it stashed."

The big find of the evening turned up in the top middle drawer, among the pens, pencils, paper clips and other miscellany. It was a smallish black ledger labeled *Memo Date Book*. For most of the recent months, during Pike's absence in South America, the pages were bare of entries. But four jotted notations from the previous fall stirred Jack's and Angie's immediate interest:

Oct 6, Sat—Lang B., Mona's Bar 7:00
Oct 8, Mon—Call other co's abt B's tip
Oct 11, Thurs—Mrs K, Staroleum, 2:30
Oct 16, Tues—XZ, 10:15

Jack Bristol looked up at the Dark Angel. "Do you read it the same way I do?"

"Probably. It seems pretty straightforward. He has a dinner or drinking date with your father on a Saturday night—during which your dad gets slightly stoned and starts telling Pike how Emerald Oil's passing up this sure strike down in Colombia. Pike then comes home to his hotel suite and jots down a reminder to call some other companies first thing Monday morning, so he can try peddling Lang Bristol's tip to them."

"Right. After which, he sees Mrs. Kenning at Staroleum on Thursday, and XZ—which has to be Xerxes Zagrevi—the following Tuesday. One of them must have come through with a deal, because there are no more such appointments listed. And by mid-December, judging from the absence of entries, he's taken off on his prospecting trip to South America."

Angie nodded agreement and started to reply—then froze as she heard someone outside the door. A key was being inserted. Jesus Christ, they'd dawdled too long! Jack gave her a look of blank panic. Angie grabbed his arm and pulled him with her to the only hiding place in reach—behind the drapes over the nearest window.

The drapery fabric must still have been trembling as they heard the door open. Luckily there was nothing in sight to give them away. The desk drawers had been closed while they studied the date book entries, and the book was now safely clutched in Angie's hand. She herself was clutched in both of Jack Bristol's hands while they flattened themselves as closely as possible against the window.

Whoever had entered was striding through the sitting room, turning left into the kitchen-dinette. He emerged again, crossing the suite. Angie peeked out just in time to see his back as he disappeared through the archway leading to the bedroom and bathroom.

"It's the bell captain!" she whispered into Jack's ear.

Seeing the lights on hadn't halted his snooping—which made it look as if he were checking for intruders on Pike's orders. He might even have been told by the desk clerk about the odd phone message and suspected it for what it was—a trick to draw Pike away from the Hotel Thermidor in case he returned too early, while some uninvited visitor was still snooping around his suite.

They could hear loud piddling from the bathroom, then the toilet flushing. A moment later the bell captain came back through the sitting room and went out, pulling the door shut behind him.

95

A silence ensued.

The Dark Angel and Jack stayed where they were behind the drapes, their hearts still beating.

"Angie?"

"Don't tell me. I know. You've got a hard-on."

"I . . . I couldn't help it . . . holding you so close."

"Who's complaining?"

"Oh, God! Would you . . . would you let me do it again?"

Angie hesitated, then drew him out from behind the drapes. "Sit down in that desk chair."

She hastily undid her suit jacket, reached behind to unhook her bra and bare her breasts. "Open your mouth." She fed them to him, one by one, and let him nurse greedily until her own juices were flowing powerfully. "AOK, baby—all systems go!"

Jack looked up at her, eager but uncertain, waiting to be prompted. "Wh–Wh–Where'll we do it?"

Angie smiled down at him. "If you mean where and how will we fuck, you tell me, honey. It's your move."

He had her pants and bikini off and his own pants down in seconds. Her arms slid around his neck while he hoisted her into a sitting position on the desk, spread her legs—and rammed.

Every stroke was an ordained and irresistible symphonic chord of heaven-and-earthly harmony. Dolce espressivo. Accelerando to presto vivace. Sforzando, crescendo. The universe exploded into ecstasy, blowing their minds completely.

For long moments neither moved, mouth to mouth, tongue to tongue, letting the great sexual tide ebb peacefully, joyously.

"I think you're getting the hang of it," whispered Angie.

"You sweet, lovely, wonderful, beautiful . . ."

"Cunt?"

"Yeah."

"Well, say it."

"Cunt!"

"Right on. Now go get me some Kleenex."

Jack Bristol slept like the dead that night in his room at the Warrick Plaza. The telephone awoke him. As he reached for it, he brought his travel alarm on the bedside stand into focus. The hands said 11:03.

"Jack?" A husky woman's voice.

"Yes . . ."

"Star Kenning."

"Oh, hi, Mrs. Kenning!"

"Did I wake you up?"

"No, no. I was just about to—to get ready for lunch."

"Good. As you know, I'm having you chaps up to my place today."

"Yes. Yes, I'm looking forward to it, Mrs. Kenning."

"So am I. But do call me Star."

"Oh, sure. Okay. Thanks, Star."

"Now look. The reason I called is this. At lunch, I'm going to announce a party for your group. It'll be there at your hotel. With girls and drinks and all. But I thought you might come back to my place, just you and I, for a little *intime* supper and—well, it'll give us a chance to get to know each other better."

"Gee, th–that sounds great, Star. But there's a friend who may be expecting me this evening."

"Now don't disappoint me, dear. After all, you and your group *are* here for discussions with Staroleum. And I *am* Staroleum. And I think you and I in particular may have a *great many* interesting things to talk over. Don't you?"

Jack suddenly remembered the entries in Laidlaw Pike's date book. "Ye–e–es. When you put it that way, I sure do, Star. Great. Let's count on it then . . . if you're sure I won't bore you."

"My dear, I hope you *will* bore me" Her voice dissolved into a peal of high-pitched silvery laughter. "Now don't ask me to explain that, darling. Ciao then."

He hung up, bounced out of bed, and opened the window curtains. The day was gorgeously sunny.

Jack Bristol showered and shaved, then phoned room service for coffee and orange juice before starting to dress. He was feeling wonderfully fit—in the mood for a hard game of handball, twenty lengths of the pool or several miles of fast-paced roadwork.

As befitted the May morning and his own high spirits, he dressed in a rakish shirt of outrageously wide blue and maroon stripes, a white cotton suit and soft white suede loafers.

It occurred to Jack as he brushed his crisp black hair into some semblance of order that he must be in love. But the word "love," the thought, the whole notion seemed irrelevant. The only important fact was that Angela Harpe was the most gorgeous creature he had ever known or imagined, and all he wanted to do for the foreseeable future was to go on kissing her and fucking her and worshiping her exquisitely beautiful bronze body as often as circumstances permitted.

With an effort, Jack remembered that he was in New York at this particular moment of his life for the express purpose of finding his father's killer.

He was drinking his coffee when a knock sounded on the door. It was Cameron Ingham—a fortyish, sun-dried stringbean of a man, assistant to Matt Yarrow, Emerald's chief of technical services.

"All set for the Dragon Lady's lunch, kid?"

"I guess. Have some coffee, Cam."

"No, thanks. I'm saving all my liquid capacity for some of Star's bonded booze."

Jack refilled his own cup. "You think Staroleum's going to buy out Emerald, Cam?"

Ingham shrugged and draped himself sideways across a chair. "Who knows? It may look as if all Star Kenning ever thinks about is cock and cocktail parties, but don't ever kid yourself, boy—that dame is one shrewd pussycat. Anyone who thinks he can read *her* mind is full of apcray."

"She hasn't done badly for a middle-aging chorus girl, that's for sure."

Ingham chuckled and lit himself a cigarette. "You can say that again, buddy boy. She marries Old Man Kenning while he's putting together his big oil combine, gets him so besotted he even names the corporation in her honor, frigs him to death in two years and winds up holding a billion-dollar pot."

Jack Bristol sipped his coffee thoughtfully. "If she's *not* planning to take over Emerald, why waste her time? What's she giving us all this red-carpet treatment for?"

"No mystery about that. She knows damn well Emerald can't negotiate any leases and start drilling till we get Fox Wineburg to float our new stock issue. Meantime, if she can con us into giving away the results of our last prospect, she might not even have to *bother* buying us out."

"If it's like that, why let her pick our brains?"

"Don't worry, kid. Doyle and Axby are no fools, either. They're willing to let us give her the company's general operating and financial picture. But when it comes to any hard data on where to drill for oil, she'll have to pay first—and pay plenty."

"She's not going to buy a pig in a poke."

"She's not going to get any free handouts, either."

"Sounds like a Mexican standoff," said Jack.

Cam Ingham nodded. "It could end up that way."

"How big a strike have we got? Or shouldn't I ask?"

Ingham laughed. "Ask away, kid. Believe it or not, I don't even know the answer myself."

"You're Matt Yarrow's assistant."

"Yeah, and that's *all* I am—his assistant. Would you believe it, there's stuff you guys sent in from the field last winter I haven't even *seen* yet. Everything goes straight to Matt. He passes on as much as he wants me to see, and no more. The rest he sits on. I'm telling you, it's the tightest security I've ever seen, in twenty years in the oil business."

Ingham stubbed out his cigarette, glanced at his wristwatch and unfolded himself from the chair. "Come on, let's get down to the lobby. It's almost a quarter past twelve. Our gilded chariots ought to be showing up pretty soon."

Jack slipped on his suitcoat, gathered up his wallet, key and loose change, and they rode down silently in a crowded elevator. As they left their keys at the desk, they saw Yarrow chatting near the front door with several other Emerald personnel. The two walked over to join them.

George Quinn, the sleek, balding, dandyfied company treasurer, grinned as he saw Jack approach. "Hey there, young fella. I hear you've been doing New York up brown."

Jack met his glance coolly. There wasn't much doubt where Quinn had gleaned his gossip, being widely regarded as a protégé of, and toady to, Wagner Axby.

The others pricked up their ears.

"Doing New York up *brown?*" Matt Yarrow repeated. "What's that supposed to mean? Has he been shoveling shit or hitting the Harlem nightspots?"

"He's been sashaying around with some real mean, lowdown colored gash," said Quinn. "And Mr. Axby don't like that, boy. Y'all going to lose your friendly support in certain quarters if you don't mend your ways."

Yarrow, thickset and freckled, rumbled a baritone chuckle. "That ain't all, kid. They tell me this black meat gets pretty rancid. You start playing tootsy-roll with some nigger whore and you could pick up a mighty painful affliction."

Bristol repressed a powerful surge of dislike. "I don't want to get stuffy, Matt, but Miss Harpe happens to be a friend of mine. Let's drop the subject."

Yarrow had tasted authority and found it too sweet to accept a put-down easily. Especially from any young punk. The kid had to be put in his place. He gathered Jack Bristol's lapel casually into his sausage-like fingers. "Don't get up on your high horse now, Jackie. When your seniors talk, you pay 'em some mind, hear? If Mr. Axby advises you to stay away from this black pig, you stay away."

"Take your hand off me." Jack spoke in a low voice, adding mentally, *you redneck sonofabitch*. Odd how a man like Wagner Axby could stamp his own personality so deeply on an organization.

Yarrow gaped in disbelief. His grip tightened on Bristol's coat and his eyes narrowed. "Now look, sonny boy. The top brass may be grooming you for the executive suite, but don't push your luck too far. Just because your old man was such a lush he got himself wasted, don't think y—"

Jack's fist slammed into his mouth, and he went staggering back against the marble wall of the lobby.

It took a few seconds for his head to clear. Conscious of muted gasps and craning onlookers, Yarrow pulled himself upright, blood oozing from his cut lip, eyes smoldering with rage.

At that moment, an elderly uniformed chauffeur

101

came into the lobby. "Excuse me, gentlemen," he said. "Are you the Emerald Oil party? Mrs. Kenning's cars are outside."

Matt Yarrow hesitated uncertainly. Then he straightened his coat and pulled out his breast-pocket handkerchief to dab the blood off his mouth.

"You cocksuckin' little pimp," he muttered to Jack Bristol. "I'll attend to you later."

Chapter Ten

Two gleaming Rolls-Royces and a Cadillac were lined up waiting at the curb. Jack straggled into the third car, conscious that Cam Ingham and most of the others were carefully dissociating themselves from him.

Fuck 'em all, he thought—a phrase Mrs. Bristol's boy was not generally in the habit of using, even to himself. Jack grinned suddenly. *Must be picking up Angie's folkways.*

He felt extraordinarily good, even with his heart still pumping and his adrenalin flow not yet throttled down. What an exquisitely satisfying thrill, belting Yarrow in the teeth! His bruised knuckles throbbed happily. Most satisfying of all, Jack knew he could do it again—in spades, if Yarrow cared to adjourn to the nearest alley. All those months of hard, sweating outdoor labor down in Colombia hadn't hardened his muscles and ironed out his gut for nothing.

The three cars tooled northward, carving their way through the midday New York traffic to Star Kenning's stately graystone townhouse on Park Avenue.

She greeted them in a tiled patio—one at a time, by name—strikingly posed beside a tinkling fountain, in a sapphire silk dress that displayed her creamy boobs at maximum visibility.

"And you, dear boy" she cooed when it came Jack's turn, pressing his hand with a hint of secret familiarity.

Champagne cocktails were served, with instant refills, after which Star led the group up a flight of marble steps to the dining room and a lunch consisting of avocado stuffed with shrimp, mixed grill and raspberry ice—washed down with a head-swimming assortment of wines.

Star Kenning sat at the head of the table with the two senior members of the Emerald group, Matt Yarrow and George Quinn, on her right and left. Both were flushed and garrulous by the time the luncheon drew to an end. Jack wondered how many nuggets of valuable information she'd extracted from them—or maybe *dis*tracted was the word, in view of her prominent mammaries.

As liqueurs followed the coffee, Star jingled a little silver bell for attention.

"As you all know, I'm just a working girl," she began —to punctual hoots of jolly laughter—"so I really must get back to the office for an hour or two *some*time this afternoon. But first I wish to make an announcement. Staroleum is throwing a party at eight this evening for you gentlemen. At your hotel, the Warrick Plaza. I'm afraid I shan't be there, since I don't want to put a damper on the festivities. But let me hasten to add that a covey of *most attractive* young ladies—from a finishing school here in New York, I'm told—or perhaps it's a riding academy—anyhow, these charmers have volunteered their services as your party hostesses and companions from *dust to dawn!*"

Enthusiastic whoops and cheering erupted, making it obvious that the alcoholic intake had weatherproofed her guests well beyond the breathalyzer danger point. Star beamed at them all.

"Now then," she went on, "even though I must be off shortly, do make yourselves completely at home here. There's a games room in the basement and a pool topside in the penthouse, where you'll find an assortment of swim trunks—that is, for anyone who doesn't care to go skinny-dipping, which is our normal custom around here." She paused coyly for an outburst of jovial masculine chuckling.

"Before I go, however, I *would* like to get to know each and every one of you just a little bit better. It occurred to me that you might care to see the art collection which my late husband and I assembled. It's really quite unusual—works which you can't see in any public museum. I thought I might take each of you through, one at a time, and in that way we'd have an opportunity to chat personally, at least for a few minutes. . . . And now, thank you all *so* much for coming to my little party."

As Star Kenning rose from the table, like a chorus girl stepping out of a birthday cake, the company rose with her for a hand-clapping ovation.

Jack saw Matt Yarrow bulldozingly capture her arm and attention—apparently asserting his claim to the first look at the Kenning art gallery. A general exodus from the dining room ensued.

Jack felt an urge to relieve his bladder. But no doubt so did most of the other guests, which meant the available toilet bowl capacity would be overstrained for the next ten minutes or so. In the interval, he found his way up to the penthouse, where he admired the luxurious blue-and-lavender tiled pool and gazed down, like stout Cortez silent upon a peak in Darien, at the teeming Manhattan traffic below.

Descending again, he homed on a room labeled LIT-TLE BOYS and leaked lengthily. Afterward he washed his hands at a sink bowl on which the mixer faucet was a gold-plated sitting girl who gushed scented water between her outspread legs when he twisted her arm or arms. Which left small doubt what the faucets looked like in the LITTLE GIRLS room.

In an alcove just off the central staircase, he noticed a telephone and on impulse dialed *A. Harpe*'s office number. His heart lifted at the sound of Angie's voice.

"This is Jack. Jack Bristol," he told her. "I'm calling from Star Kenning's townhouse."

"Lucky you!"

"That's debatable, but never mind. Look, here's what I called about, Angie. I was hoping to see you this evening—if not sooner—but something's come up." He told her about the party which Star Kenning was laying on for the Emerald Oil group at the Hotel Warrick, and his own private invitation to return to Star's townhouse for an intimate supper.

"Repeat—lucky you," chuckled the Dark Angel.

"Repeat—that's debatable. But anyhow, I wasn't going to accept, and then I remembered that entry we saw in Laidlaw Pike's date book last night."

There was a momentary silence. "You sure this phone's safe?" said Angie.

"How do you mean, safe?"

"Nobody listening. Not bugged."

"Well, fairly sure. There must be twenty phones in the joint, judging from the scale of everything else around here. I doubt if she'd have them all monitored."

"Okay. Go on."

"Well, if Dad's murder had anything to do with Colombian oil," said Jack, "so far we've turned up three connections. There's Pike himself, who we know got a

106

tip from Dad and who has since staged a prospecting expedition of his own in the same area. And then there are also the two people he tried to interest in Dad's tip—Mrs. Kenning and Xerxes Zagrevi. Well, this supper tonight will give me a chance to find out what if anything developed from her talk with Pike."

"Hmm, you may have something there," Angie said thoughtfully. "Just for the sake of argument—going back to your original theory—who if anyone in that Emerald Oil group would you call the likeliest suspect?"

Jack Bristol pondered her question. "Number one—Matt Yarrow. To be honest, I don't like the bastard, which probably colors my judgment. But he used to work under Dad, and now he's advanced to chief of technical services, which is fairly high up in the company hierarchy. So I suppose you could say that gives him a motive right there. Also, next to Dad, he's the one who had the most access to the original field data from that first expedition."

"Matt Yarrow, huh?" Angie sounded as if she were jotting down the name.

"Right. Next to him, I'd say George Quinn, who's the company treasurer. No solid reason for naming Quinn, except that he's—well, what I'd call a manipulator by nature, and he knows all the financial ins and outs of the company. Also, he's very ambitious and obviously looking out for numero uno."

Jack turned abruptly, sensing rather than hearing someone close behind him. A sleek blond butler had come up on silent feet.

"George Quinn, okay. One more thing," said Angie. "Did you by chance notice an entry in Pike's date book about someone named—"

"Excuse me a second," Jack interrupted. "I think someone wants to speak to me." He lowered the phone and gave the butler a coldly questioning look. "Yes?"

"Excuse me, sir, but Mrs. Kenning would like to see you in her art salon."

"Where is that?"

"I believe she's expecting me to show you the way, sir." There was a faint, almost imperceptible, glint of amusement in the butler's eyes as if he were enjoying Jack's uncertainty as to whether or not he'd been overheard.

Jack spoke into the phone. "Let me call you back later." He hung up and turned suddenly—in such a way as to step with his full weight on the butler's glossily polished shoe. "Oh! I'm so sorry!"

In stony silence the butler led him to a double-doored archway on one side of a vast sitting room, and knocked. When Star Kenning's voice said, "Come in," he slid apart the doors and stood aside for Jack Bristol to enter.

"Darling," Star said, coming up to take his hands, "it's so nice to get you alone! I especially wanted *you* to see my treasures before I have to rush off."

Two of her treasures were already on ample display. But Jack abstained from the obvious comment and responded with conventionally polite noises.

The room was parquet-floored with graceful love seats and benches from which to view the framed canvases that lined its green baize walls.

"I shan't bore you with these masterpieces," Star said, smiling. She named and pointed out with a casual sweep of her arm a Jackson Pollock, a Utrillo, a George Bellows, a Modigliani, a Claude Monet, a Georgia O'Keefe, a Salvador Dali, a large sun-dappled Mary Cassatt and a Jasper Johns.

Jack Bristol knew just enough about painting to estimate, slightly dazed, that the collection must represent at least a cool two or three million.

But Star Kenning was already taking his arm, turning

his attention to half a dozen paintings on the wall behind them. Each was a lifesize portrait of herself done, if not by a master, certainly by an artist-craftsman of the most superb technical competence. Star in riding habit astride a thoroughbred hunter; Star on the grass like Christina; Star in fetching tennis costume returning a serve; Star on a chaise longue; Star in a ball gown as she might have posed for Whistler or John Singer Sargent; Star barefoot with windswept hair on a lonely beach.

"Which do you like best, darling?" said Star.

"How can I choose?" Jack stalled. "But if you force me . . . well, perhaps this one on the chaise longue."

"You *devil!*" Star squeezed his arm delightedly. "You *knew!*"

"Knew what?" said Jack, perplexed.

By way of answer, Star produced a tiny plastic device like a transistor radio of matchbox size, with a correspondingly tiny antenna. She turned the dial, then pressed the knob.

The portrait on the chaise longue rotated 180 degrees through the wall. On its back was a portrait of identical size. In this one, however, Star was starkers—a modern Naked Maja, but somewhat less modest in pose than the original Duchess of Alba, since her pelvis was turned toward the viewer and one knee raised to reveal a hairy crotch in breathtaking detail.

"Quite *trompe-l'oeil,* wouldn't you say?" giggled Star.

"Uh, gosh, yes. It'd not only fool *my* eye, it might even *blind* a fellow. It's absolutely dazzling!" Jack smiled valiantly to conceal his slightly shocked feeling. After all, the woman was probably old enough to be his mother, even if she did look no more than thirty-five. One fancied one could almost discern her clitoris peeping out through the underbrush. "You mean I—I actually managed to pick the one portrait with this, uh—*revelation* behind it?"

"Unerringly, darling! . . . Oh, there *are* nudie pix behind my other portraits, too. But with this one you hit the bull's-eye as it were!" Star burst into a peal of laughter which was perhaps a trifle more metallic than silvery. "Would you like to see the others?"

"Dare I?"

"For your eyes only, luv! If the other members of your group only knew!"

Fleetingly, Jack found himself wondering about that. But Star was twirling and pressing the dial knob—again and yet again. Each time, another portrait revolved, until a half-dozen naked, lifesize Mrs. Kennings stared back at them from the green-baize wall. The effect was overpowering. A naked Star forking a white stallion; Star sunbathing on the lawn; Star tit-flopping as she ran down a tennis smash; Star showing all; Star with fan, gloves and high heels; Star rising from the foam like Aphrodite.

"Wow! What can one say?" said Jack, wondering what to say.

"Say nothing, sweetie. Not a word to anyone, mind! Just look for my Rolls at eight sharp outside the Warrick Plaza."

Jack was startled speechless as he felt Star's fingers suddenly tweak his genitalia. "Who knows, darling?" she murmured in his ear. "Play your cards right, and tonight you might even see the real thing!"

Chapter Eleven

The Dark Angel hung up from Jack Bristol's phone call feeling annoyed and frustrated. Not so much at the interruption as at being unable to recall the entry in Pike's date book which kept nagging at the back of her mind.

She couldn't even be sure about the name—*Hardy, Underwood,* something like that. What had caught her eye was the wording of the entry, its implied urgency. Dammit, the whole bit remained teasingly out of reach, just below her level of consciousness.

All Angie knew for sure was that it had sounded promising—as if it might offer a key to Pike's actions. She'd been just about to draw Jack Bristol's attention to it there in Laidlaw Pike's hotel suite when the damned bell captain came barging in.

And then Jack's hard-on, plus ensuing developments, had driven the whole thing from her mind.

Oh, well. Angela Harpe grinned. Her tissues still glowed from last night's coupling on Pike's desk. Talk about having a ball!

Meanwhile, moving on to this party Star Kenning had laid on tonight for the Emerald Oil dudes—it sounded like an interesting opportunity to fish for information.

Not the way Angie usually chose to fish these days, but still . . . why pass it up?

She flipped through a little leather directory in her desk drawer and dialed a phone number. Listened to the ringing at the other end until a female voice answered.

"Hello?"

"Carol?"

"You've got her."

"This is Angie."

"*Angie!* Hey, how about that!"

"Still in the game?"

"What else? Still waiting for my millionaire. . . . How about you? Still crime-busting?"

"For money, honey. Strictly for money."

"Smart gal!"

"Look," said Angie. "You doing any corporate work these days? Or just catering to your own little charmed circle of steadies?"

"Oh, no. I'm on call to about half a dozen PR firms and corporations. In fact I average three or four nights a week that way."

"Freelance, right?"

"You know it, sweetie. Why split the take?" said the girl called Carol.

"Who's handling the big accounts these days? I mean the sales meetings and conventions—stuff like that."

"Oh, you know, same old operators who specialize in the executive-suite trade. I guess about the biggest pimp on the business circuit is still Longdong. . . . Remember him?"

"I'll say I do," said Angie in tones redolent with dislike. "Longdong Strong. That motherfuckin' gorilla!"

Carol chuckled. "The dear old ACM. Matter of fact I had a call from him this morning. Wanted me for a job."

112

"Staroleum?"

"Now how the hell did you know that?" said Carol, genuinely impressed. "Hey, you're really on the ball with this private eye shit!"

"What did you tell him?"

"The polite equivalent of fuck you, nigger. Mind you, I don't object to turning a trick on call now and then for a suede pimp. Matter of fact, it was a black stud who first turned me out. But not Longdong Strong. Him I don't mess around with, if I can help it. He's a ha–a–a–ard mack!"

"How come he called? Is he out of girls from his own stable?"

"Yeah, business is booming, I guess. He needed about a dozen ladies for a party tonight at the Warrick Plaza, and he was still short one stick. But I've already got a date, one of my steadies. I told him to try Moira Cane."

"Think she took the job?" asked Angie.

"Yeah, probably. I gave her a ring to let her know he might call. She said sure—she had an open book tonight."

The Dark Angel chatted a while longer, made a vague lunch date for the following week. Her onyx eyes were thoughtful as she put down the phone. Longdong Strong was a bad nigger to mess with. Not for nothing was he known in The Life as the Abominable Cunt Man. He'd cut more broads than Vidal Sassoon.

On the other hand, if she knew Moira, it wouldn't be too hard to maneuver a switch. And Angie did know Moira.

Once again the Dark Angel took out her little leather directory. This time, the number she dialed was Moira Cane's.

"Angie, darling! What's up?"

113

"Oh, nothing special. Just felt like rapping, so I got out my little black book to see who I could call. . . . Bit lonesome, I guess. . . . You busy?"

"Heck, no. Come on over. I'm feeling kinda lonesome myself. Maybe we can cheer each other up."

"Okay. You still on East 62nd?"

"Sure, same place. Apartment 58. I'll tell the doorman you're coming."

Angie got a small bottle of pills out of her desk drawer, shook two into her palm, and tucked them into the little coin pocket of her denim skirt. Leaving the office, she stopped at a liquor store down the street and bought a bottle of Sabra.

A cab dropped her in front of Moira Cane's apartment building. The doorman, who didn't like spades but couldn't help approving of a stone fox like the Dark Angel, gave her a grudgingly lustful smile and buzzed apartment 58 to let Moira know her guest had arrived.

"Okay, you can go right on up," he told Angie.

Moira Cane was a college girl from Toledo, who was working in fits and starts on a master's in English Lit at NYU while she earned ten times the average prof's salary with her natural talents. A curvy honey blonde, she was wearing nothing but her hair as she opened the door to Angie.

"Darling! I'm so glad you came!" She flung her arms around the Dark Angel and kissed her on the lips. "I was just flaked out in bed, watching my favorite soap opera. . . . Hey, what've you got there?"

Angie pulled the bottle of Sabra out of the paper bag.

"Oooh, goodie! My favorite booze! Come on in and join me!"

Moira led the way into her boudoir, which had walls upholstered in white vinyl, a circular bed and ceiling mirror, and what looked like wall-to-wall carpeting of

114

polar bear fur. On her bedside liquor cabinet was a half-empty box of chocolates.

"Help 'self, honey." Moira gestured to the candy and flung herself onto the bed. "And then how about mixing us some of those yummy guzzles you're so good at?"

"Any soda?"

"Sure—plenty out in the fridge."

Angie got ice and glasses, and mixed orange and chocolate soda and sabra and vodka in a shaker.

"Oooh, wow! Is that ever good!" exclaimed Moira, gulping at her drink greedily. "I don't know why I don't get fat, I'm such a pig."

"Whatever kind of diet you're on, honey, just keep it up," said Angie. "You must be doing something right."

Moira smiled at her.

On the second round, Angie went to get more ice. This time she did the pouring in the kitchen and managed to slip the two pills into Moira's glass.

Moira lounged on her pillows, dividing her attention between TV, her drink and Angie. Mostly she looked at Angie.

"Working tonight?" asked the Dark Angel.

"Uh-huh. Party at the Warrick Plaza. Lulu Easton's gonna pick me up at seven-thirty. . . . Wish I didn't have to go, though, now that you're here."

They sipped their drinks for a while.

"How about coming up here with me?" said Moira as the day's installment of soapsuds and tears faded from the television screen, giving way to the closing commercial.

"Sure, if you insist." Angie got up from the luxuriously comfy overstuffed chair she'd been curled in, kicked off her heels and stretched out on the sheets beside Moira.

The blonde call girl gathered the Dark Angel into her

arms. Angie didn't mind. There were times when a woman's body felt more comforting to embrace than a man's. And it was kinda groovy at that, bumping titties with a fellow female. Especially a female with titties like Moira Cane's.

On impulse, Angie lowered her head and kissed both of them on their pink nipples.

"Oh, God!" said Moira, closing her eyes. She embraced Angie more tightly for a few moments. "Would you mind if I went down on you?"

Angie smiled. "To quote you—'Help 'self, honey!' "

Moira squirmed around to focus her attention on Angie's pelvic area. She hiked up the brief little skirt, then made a face. "Oh, shit! You would be wearing a body shirt. Take it off, huh?"

Angie complied, stripping to the buff. Moira knelt on the bed with her face between Angie's thighs and ate avidly. Angie shivered and moaned with delight at her expert ministrations.

Finally Moira looked up from the honey pot, her mouth dripping. "Please, darling! Would you sixty-nine me?"

"My pleasure, sweetie."

Moira reversed herself to Angie, and the Dark Angel put her head between the honey blonde's legs. Moira screamed as Angie's tongue touched her clit, and writhed in ecstasy at the lapping follow-through. Both girls went into repeated orgasms.

At last Moira rolled over, exhausted and bathed in sweat. She lay panting a while, her breasts heaving, then pulled herself up to lie with her face on the pillows beside Angie's. She kissed the black girl tenderly.

"I love you, Angie."

Moments later, she was asleep.

Angie waited until she was sure Moira Cane was deep in dreamland. Then she got out of bed, padded into the bathroom and ran the shower. The cool pelting droplets on her skin felt heavenly.

Afterward, she wiped and patted herself dry with a towel as soft and fluffy as a merino sheep fleece. It was fun sampling Moira's powders and scents. Wafting a potpourri of fragrance, the Dark Angel went into the kitchen, still naked, and made herself some Earl Grey tea.

The time was 5:17. Over two hours to wait. No danger of Moira waking up. With those sleeping pills in her, on top of the alcohol and sex, she was probably out till morning. But for Angie, the wait was bound to be a bit of a bore.

Still, it was fun making herself at home in another girl's apartment. Especially feeling as good as she did right now. Angie took her tea into the living room, selected an annotated copy of Malory's *Morte d'Arthur* from the bookcase and settled down to pass the time.

An hour and a half later, she decided she'd better get ready. Too bad she hadn't stopped at her own pad for a better choice of clothes before coming to Moira's. But there was plenty to fit her in the blonde call girl's extravagantly bountiful wardrobe.

Angie chose some wispy pink lace panties, garter belt and stockings, and geared in these—with an erotic excuse for a bra—finally settled on a delicious little cocktail dress of shimmering ivory silk. Fortunately, her own white heels would go beautifully with the outfit.

Shortly before 7:30 the buzzer sounded.

"Some ladies here in a car for Miss Cane," the doorman reported. Another break. Judging from his voice, a different doorman had come on duty—so he wouldn't even be aware of Angie's change in costume.

"Okay. Ask them to wait a minute, please."

Angie went down in the elevator and out into the twilight to find a big pink Thunderbird at the curb, full of

117

eye-catching hookers. All were white except for an exotic houri whom Angie recognized as a Chinese-Chicano named Blossom Castilla. At the wheel was Lulu Easton, a top ho in Longdong's stable.

"Where the hell is Moira?" she asked Angie.

"Up in bed, copping Zs. Her period came on early. She got the cramps so bad, she had to take a couple of pills. You want a substitute?"

"You?" Lulu had known Angie slightly when the lovely black girl was fashion-modeling and on call after graduating from Radcliffe, but she had no notion of Angie's subsequent career. She looked the Dark Angel over with a vague, worried frown.

"What you sees is what you get, dear," said Angie.

With a violently sadistic boss like Longdong, Lulu had little experience of, or taste for making decisions on her own. On the other hand, she did need a girl—and Longdong would sure as hell lay some coathanger on her if she loused up the party in any way, since the night's contract was probably bringing him a good ten Gs.

"How much you want?"

"Shit, don't worry about that," said Angie. "I'm just doing it for Moira. She can slip me a cut of whatever Longdong promised her."

"Okay, hop in."

At the Warrick Plaza, the bell captain had an attendant in street clothes waiting to garage the Thunderbird while the girls slipped discreetly into the hotel. They were whisked up by the service elevator to a private dining room on the tenth floor. Here they joined the rest of the girls, who had arrived in a separate car driven by Flora Wing, a slender, hot-eyed high yellow. Flora, almost light-skinned enough to pass, was Longdong Strong's "bottom lady"—the queen of his stable.

"What the fuck are you doing here, Angie?" she asked in a voice as friendly as an electric drill.

"Filling in for Moira, dear. Any objection?"

Lulu hastened to explain, a trifle nervously, what had happened to the honey blonde call girl.

"And you just taking her place out of the kindness of your heart, huh?" Flora regarded Angie with brittle dislike. She had never trusted this high-sidin' broad since the first time they met—recognizing her enviously as one outlaw with enough game in her to play past any obstacle that life, the law or the urban jungle might toss in her path.

Angie's expression hardened. "Make up your mind, sister. You want me or don't you? If not, I'll split."

Inwardly she wondered if Flora had heard of her role as the Dark Angel.

The question was brushed aside as the dining room doors suddenly opened and the Emerald Oil men came surging in.

"Okay, stick around," Flora snapped to Angie. Switching on a sexy smile, the bottom lady turned to greet the party guests as they paused to look over the girls.

"Hey, get a load of that, Matt," said a balding man in a sleekly tailored silk sharkskin suit. "There's some of that dark meat you were warning the kid about."

Angie saw him address the remark to a biggish, freckle-faced, heavy-jawed dude who looked like a pro tackle gone to seed. So this was Matt Yarrow. They were both looking straight at her—ignoring Flora, who was already steering the others toward various girls of her group.

"Did I hear a call for dark meat?" Angie came ankling up to them, swaying her hips provocatively, her eyes on Yarrow.

"You sho'nuff did, honey chile—and I'm the one who's doin' the callin'!" He slipped an arm around her, one hand reaching beneath her armpit to squeeze the side of her breast.

"Fast work," said George Quinn. "Looks like I better go cut me one out of the herd."

A bar had been set up in one corner of the room while the buffet dinner was laid out, and a stereo hi-fi player began blaring soul-rock over the wall speakers.

Angie and Matt Yarrow got drinks and hors-d'-oeuvres and drew aside for some verbal foreplay.

Angie began rubbing her rump sensuously against the wall with a pained expression. "Oooh, my right cheek itches!" she whispered. "But I *must* be ladylike—and, besides, my hands are full. Would you be a sweetheart and scratch it for me?"

"Just leave it to your old Uncle Matt, baby!" Yarrow reached around up her skirt and inside her panties to knead and pinch her bare buttock. "Man, oh man!" he muttered, his face slowly reddening. "Like they say on TV, it's the real thing! So round, so firm, so fully packed!"

Angie dimpled. "I said scratch, not feel, Daddy."

"So you did, honey chile. So you did." He scratched briefly, but soon went back to palping and caressing. "Look, why the hell are we wasting time on this dinner jazz? Why don't we go have some fun? We can always come back and stuff our guts later. Right now I'd rather be stuffing you."

"I *do* like a man who knows his own mind, Daddy. Let's blast off."

Two minutes later Yarrow had her clamped in a slobbering bear hug in his room.

"Hey, cool it, man! Let's do this thing right," she said, pushing him away gently but firmly.

120

"I'll do it right, baby—don't worry about that. Just flop down and spread your legs."

"Shit no, lover. I'm going to see to it that this is a night you'll remember. Now just you relax and talk and leave everything to little ole honey chile."

"Who the fuck wants to talk when you're around, baby?" Yarrow grinned and cupped her ass with both hands. But he let her slip off his suitcoat and stood still amiably while she began undoing his tie and unbuttoning his shirt.

"I don't even know your name," she whispered. "Did I hear that other dude call you Matt?"

"That's me, baby. What do they call you?"

"Angie."

"Hey, I like that."

"You'll like what's coming even better. . . . You some kind of salesman, Matt honey? What's your line?"

"Me, I'm in the oil business."

"Oil business? No kidding? I knew a dude once in the oil business. He was one of my regular boyfriends."

"Yeah? Who was that? John D. Rockefeller?"

"Shit no, smartass. His name was Lang Bristol."

"Lang Bristol!" Angie could feel Yarrow's body stiffen, saw his eyes flare with interest and a hint of suspicion. "Are you bullshittin' me? I knew Bristol. He worked for the same outfit I do."

"Honest?" Angie widened her own eyes in innocent, hopeful surprise. "Then where's he keeping himself, man? Jeez, I haven't seen him or heard from him since last year."

"It'll be a hell of a lot longer than that before you hear from him again, baby. He's dead."

"Dead!" Angie let her arms drop to her sides. "You're not jiving me?"

"Hell, no. Someone shot him."

121

"Well, I'll be double goddamned. Why would anyone go and do a thing like that to a sweet old dude like him?"

"I dunno, and who gives a fuck, anyhow? Let's get on with the dance, baby!"

"Yeah, I guess that's what we're here for, ain't it?" The Dark Angel continued undressing Yarrow and pushed him down in a chair while she pulled off his pants and shorts. Kneeling at his feet for a moment, she began fondling his genitals. "Old Lang, he used to tell me how he went hunting for oil. What do you do, Daddy? Drill the wells?"

"Nah, that's work for the hardhats." Yarrow gasped and chuckled with pleasure as she gave him a few teasing licks and sucks. "Me, I show 'em *where* to drill."

"Yeah. Well, I'll show *you* where to drill in a minute, Daddy. Meantime, you just sit right there and keep talking."

Angie drew away from him slightly and pulled up the skirt of the ivory silk mini-dress to give him a good view of her wispy pink panties. She began to turn slowly, revolving and grinding her hips as she did so.

"How come you're so smart about where to dig wells, Daddy?" she crooned. "You struck any oil lately?"

She was inserting her thumbs inside the waistband as if to start peeling off the panties, when someone knocked on the door.

"Who the hell is that?" Yarrow grunted irritably.

"It's important, Mr. Yarrow," said a Negro voice. "I'm here for Mrs. Kenning. Can I rap with you a minute?"

"All right, hang on," Yarrow grumbled. He hastily began pulling on his clothes. "Okay, let the dumb bastard in, Angie, so I can get rid of him. Then we'll get down to business."

Angie turned the knob. Instantly the door was

slammed wide open and two hard-looking bloods stepped into the room. Each was holding a gun.

"Now, w—w—wait a minute! What the hell is this all about?" spluttered Matt Yarrow.

"Cool it, Mr. Yarrow. Nuthin to do with you," said one.

"It's this no-good jiveass broad we're after."

Chapter Twelve

"She may be a no-good jiveass broad to you, brother, but she's my piece of party ass tonight!" growled Matt Yarrow, recovering his normal bluster at the black's respectful tone. "Come on now! What's this all about?"

"She ain't no ho, she a private eye—that's what it's all about, Charlie!" the other blood blurted contemptuously.

"A private eye?" echoed Yarrow. His jaw dropped in dismay and his glance shifted to Angie.

"Yeah, man. She just muscled in on the party to make chumps outa you dudes and see what she could find out. She probably working for some other oil company. Naturally Mrs. Kenning ain't gon' let nuthin like that happen to her guests."

"Why, you goddamn little bitch!" Yarrow exploded at Angie. "So that's why you were pumping me for information! I oughta bust your fuckin' jaw!"

"Don't worry, man. This bitch gon' get her ass kicked upside her head where we takin' her. But that don't mean you gotta do without pussy tonight—we brought you along a real foxy replacement."

The speaker opened the door and beckoned someone inside with a jerk of his head. A curly-haired platinum

124

blonde entered, looking as if she might have stepped straight out of the pages of *Playboy* Magazine.

"He—e—e—ey, now that's what I call service!" said Yarrow. "Come on in, baby, let's get to know each other. What kinda little girl are you?"

The platinum blonde giggled, unzipped herself and stepped out of her red dress in approximately two seconds, revealing a brace of oversized mammaries and an unbleached crotch. "I'm *this* kinda little girl, lover. . . . You like?"

Yarrow chuckled deeply and reached out. "Do I ever, baby!"

"Just be sure you warn him about your chancre, Patsy dear," said Angie. "And don't let any germs rub off where they might have to amputate."

The platinum blonde turned on her in fury, and Angie saw Matt Yarrow's face pale in sudden apprehension, just before one of the black gunmen slapped her across the ear with his piece.

"Outside, bitch!"

The Dark Angel had never seen either of the two gunsels before, but no introductions were needed. She recognized their style on sight. A couple of ice-cold young dudes in broad-brimmed mack hats, sharp suits and high-heeled boots—just aching to show their stuff. And they didn't give a fuck about silencers.

They made her walk down the center of the corridor while one trailed her on each side. The dude left rear was toting a cheap Saturday Night Special—the other a Russian or Chinese Tokarev pistol, which he must have picked up in Vietnam. No use even toying with the idea of any sudden aikido twirl or karate kick. These were two badass niggers with nothing to lose. One false move and they'd blow her full of holes and take their chances on getting out of the hotel alive.

Someone was holding open the door of the service elevator at the end of the hall. It was a black hotel maid. The dude with the Tokarev pinched the maid's ass as they shepherded Angie aboard. "Take it down, Mama. This chick's got a date uptown with Longdong Strong —and he sure don't like to be kep' waiting."

"Mrs. Kenning is waiting on the roof, sir," said the sleek blond butler. "She thought you might find a swim in the pool refreshing before supper."

His lips twitched in a faint poisonous smile.

Jack Bristol rode up in the lift uneasily. He had been picked up outside the Warrick Plaza in Star's Silver Phantom Rolls ten minutes before, conscious of certain doubts about the wisdom of having accepted her invitation. The doubts were rapidly growing to a certainty as he recalled her remark at the luncheon table about the customary swimming costume in her penthouse pool.

To his relief, however, she was reclining gracefully in a deck chair in a reasonably modest bikini. The only slightly unnerving note was her bushy underarm hair.

"Darling, I'm *so* glad you could join me tonight," she said, seizing Jack's hand. "Do my armpits shock you? I only let them grow out because someone told me men find it erotic. . . . Do you? . . . Oh well, never mind, darling, I can see you're bashful. You'll find scads of swim trunks in the boys' locker room over there. Do hurry up and change!"

A few minutes later they were larking in the water. Star was a remarkably accomplished swimmer, although Jack was somewhat disconcerted by her habit of suddenly diving between his legs.

"There's one thing I haven't told you, dear," she said with a mischievous smile as she broke water like a sleekly surfacing seal.

"What's that?" asked Jack.

"These swimsuits we have on . . ."

"What about them?"

"They're knit from a new synthetic fiber developed by one of our Staroleum subsidiaries."

"Oh? What sort of fiber?"

"It's water soluble."

Jack gulped and suddenly realized why his trunks seemed so lightweight. As he gaped in confusion, he saw that Star's bikini, too, was slowly dissolving before his eyes.

They continued swimming for a while longer in the balmy night air under the moonlit Manhattan sky, but conversation lagged. Star kept embracing him in the water. Jack was disinclined to respond, but felt idiotic when he passively allowed himself to be caressed.

"Silly boy!" giggled Star. "Come on, I think we're relaxed enough by now, don't you? Let's have supper."

They climbed out of the pool.

"Er, let me just go and dress first," pleaded Jack as she took his hand

"If you insist, darling. . . . May I watch?"

As it turned out, his clothes had disappeared.

"The butler must have taken them," said Star. "Now that I think of it, I believe I did tell him to carry them downstairs after you changed. One of my silly feminine whims! It seemed such a fun idea, us dressing together in my boudoir."

Her boudoir was an incredible extravaganza in ice-cream pastel tones and textures ranging from satin and deep-pile shag to leather and glass.

Star plopped down at her dressing table and fastened a black velvet choker—studded with either diamonds or very large rhinestones—around her neck.

"My, uh, clothes don't seem to be here," said Jack after a brief, unsuccessful search.

"No?" Star looked around vaguely. "Never mind. We'll ask Ventnor when he brings in the food. In the meantime, would you lend me a hand, darling?"

From an open drawer overflowing with frothy femininities, she pulled out what looked like an oddly narrow black satin corset. As she wrapped it around herself, Jack saw that it extended from several inches below her ample breasts to barely over her navel. "It's called a waist cincher, dear. Just zip it up in back. Do you like it?"

Turning around to face him after he got the zipper closed, she went on, "Now tell me honestly, Jack—do you find stockings erotic the way most men seem to?"

"Why, uh . . . I don't know that I ever gave it much thought, Star."

"Of course you have, darling. But I suppose you're too shy and inhibited to discuss it. . . . Oh well, I suppose I may as well go whole hog." She proceeded to pull on a pair of filmy black nylons and fasten them to the long garters of her waist cincher. "I've always assumed the effect must have something to do with the contrast between the dark stocking tops and one's white thighs. You know—hinting at the ultimate disclosure." She gave one of her familiar peals of silvery laughter as she slipped her feet into spike-heeled black pumps.

Speaking of ultimate disclosures, Jack found it hard to avoid noticing her extreme profusion of dark pubic hair. Apparently her armpits weren't the only thing Star allowed to grow out.

"Well! Shall we eat now?" Star pressed a button on her dressing table, adding with a giggle, "And kindly notice I did *not* mean by 'eat' what you thought I meant, you naughty boy!"

The blond butler promptly wheeled in an enormous serving cart as if he'd been waiting outside the door.

"Ventnor, what did you do with Mr. Bristol's clothes?"

128

"I thought he might like them cleaned and pressed, madam." He darted a one-thousandth-of-a-second smile of barbed spite at Jack. "They seemed rather in need of attention. I shall have them laid out for him next door."

"Splendid. That will do now, Ventnor."

The covered wells of the serving cart were filled with a delicious variety of dishes. But Jack had lost most of his appetite under the bland gaze of the butler. Star, however, seemed utterly unembarrassed at being seen by a servant in her partial state of dress, or undress.

With an effort of will, Jack forced himself to concentrate on his reason for coming to this fantastic supper.

"How are your, uh, negotiations coming along with Emerald Oil, Star?"

She shrugged carelessly. "Who knows? Wagner Axby's such an incredible crook and con man! Of course, don't let on that I told you so, darling. But even *my* accountants can't make head or tail of his books—and, believe me, they're the best money can buy!"

She smiled maternally at Jack. "How would you like it if I bought Emerald Oil and made you president? . . . I could, you know. And you wouldn't have to do a thing—just sit at a big imposing desk and look as handsome as you do now! . . . Oooh, you do look so yummy, darling, with that flat stomach and those hard chest muscles and that deep tan, and all that black fuzzy hair from your neck on down!"

Jack flushed with confusion and tried hard to ignore the fact that Star herself was looking exceptionally attractive for a woman her age. Whatever the heck that might be. All that creamy bare flesh, the pinkish brown nipples, the wanton disarray of long, raven-dark hair, even if its color doubtless did owe something to the dyer's art. In short, such sheer sexy opulence—especially in that cathouse costume!

"Tell me something, Star"—forcing his attention back

to business. "How much do you know about Laidlaw Pike?"

She was silent a moment, staring at him curiously. "Laidlaw Pike? . . . Why do you ask, dear?"

Jack attempted a casual shrug. "They say he's made a strike down in Colombia, too. If you're looking for a new oil field, why not buy *him* out, rather than Emerald? . . . Has he ever approached you?"

Star's face took on a tolerant smile. "So that's why you accepted my invitation tonight. . . . Oh, don't worry! I don't mind in the slightest as long as you're here. I might even answer your question, dear—if you make the right kind of impression."

Jack felt a pang of alarm. He was barely picking at his food, and Star too seemed ready to abandon the meal. Possibly for more interesting endeavors.

"Let's go look for those clothes of yours, Jackie luv."

She took him by the hand and led him through a doorway into the adjoining room. It was perfectly circular, with walls, ceiling and floor entirely of glass, reflecting back a bewildering infinity of images.

In the center of the room was a large white leather hassock, with a slender black snakelike object lying across it. The object proved on closer inspection to be a braided belt or leash with a silver snap-hook on one end and a looped handle on the other.

Star pressed a button somewhere on the hassock, and the room echoed with a rollicking band march.

"Recognize that tune, darling?" Jack shook his head. "It was quite well-known at one time—a Boston Pops sort of thing—but perhaps you're too young to recall. It's 'The Whistler and His Dog.' Quite charming, don't you think?"

The music was interspersed with gay whistles and barks.

"I, uh, don't seem to see my clothes around," Jack remarked.

"Do stop worrying about them, darling. I'll make sure you leave here fully dressed." As she spoke, Star attached the hook end of the braided leash to a small silver ring at the back of her diamond velvet choker.

Another volley of barks interrupted the music.

She handed the free end of the leash to Jack, who stared at her uneasily.

"You do want an answer, darling, to your question about Laidlaw Pike?"

"Er, yes. I would appreciate knowing that, Star."

"Good! I see no reason why we can't exchange favors. But first, as the kennel phrase goes—she knelt down on all fours on the hassock and presented her white backside to Jack—"how would you like to stand at stud?"

Chapter Thirteen

The two black gunsels had taken Angie to Longdong Strong's crib up on Sugar Hill. And now she was strung up, high and dry, on his famous four-poster—the bed where Longdong had personally broken in more chicks, most of them white, than any other boss player in the game.

His goons, Snake Man and Leroy, had ripped off her ivory silk dress and her pink panties and bra without a blink of interest in her lovely bronze body. They were both training hard to get their front up tight as boss pimps like Longdong—stone cold players with a gut-deep hatred for women—the kind who look on female genitals strictly as moneymakers and give up no sex of their own except for cash or in reward for tricks turned.

Angie's ankles were lashed to the tops of the posts at the foot of the bed and her wrists were tied to the other bed legs—so that she was spread-eagled with her crotch high and her head low.

Longdong paid her no mind. He had taken out the folded thousand dollar bill in which he kept his cocaine, and was delicately snuffing up the white "jam" off a little jeweled spoon which he carried on a platinum chain around his neck.

He was a huge, bull-necked Negro with skin like elephant hide. His only visible hair was a black goatee, waxed to curve outward like a hook. He was sporting amethyst-lensed pimp shades, an elaborate silk dressing gown specially embroidered for him in Hong Kong with sinister blue and green dragons, black velvet tights and plum-colored knee boots.

He threw back his head, inhaled deeply and pocketed his jam. "Well, bitch. You ready to talk?"

"What the hell am I supposed to talk about?" said Angie.

"You know where I'm coming from, woman. Just run down yo' game for me, that's all I ask. Lay a little truth on me."

"I've already told you—Moira had menstrual cramps."

"Correction, trick baby. That's what you done told Flora and she phoned word to me—'cause she be right down taking care of business, like the righteous lady she is. But this is Longdong Strong you talking to now—Longdong, the Abominable Cunt Man. So don't try coming on with that kinda jive."

"Well, it's the truth, whether you buy it or not," Angie retorted stubbornly. "Moira had cramps, so I offered to stand in for her."

"Bullshit, you sidity bitch. You ain't peddled pussy since the day you joined the fuzz—and even before then you weren't ever really in The Life. Just an outlaw, that's all you ever was, trying to game your way up past the real working chicks. So why should you start turning tricks now, just for some dumb-ass motherfuckin' broad like Moira?"

"Okay, man. You know so much, you tell me."

"I'ma do more'n *tell* you, bitch. I'ma beat yo' fuckin' moneymaker till you piss blood." Longdong picked up his "pimp sticks"—two wire coathangers twisted togeth-

133

er—and slapped them against his huge ivory-skinned palm. "You always was strong for signification. But I must be feeling extra kind tonight. 'Cause I'ma give you one more chance. You care to tell me what you was after?"

Angie sketched a futile shrug.

Whooosh! The pimp sticks whistled through the air between her up-stretched legs. Her mound and vulva felt like they had just been slammed with a red-hot poker.

Whooosh! She almost cried out with pain.

"One more chance, bitch. I'm hip to this Dark Angel shit, and you know I'm hip."

Whooosh!

"That mean someone was paying you to private-eye on them oil dudes, prob'ly trying to beat that Kenning broad's time."

Whooosh!

"But Staroleum's one of my steady customers, dig? And I don't like my business rep besmirched by any of that private-eye shit you try'na pull. Y'understand what I'm saying?"

Whooosh!

"Now. You ready to lay the truth on me, or you freaking for more coathanger?"

Angie's brain revved wildly. By arching her body, then sinking down at the very instant the pimp sticks landed, she had managed to take some of the sting out of the blows. But it was getting past that point now. Her genitals were on fire.

Maybe she should spill her guts. After all, what did it matter if she broke down and told him Jack Bristol had hired her? It was hardly all that much of a secret. Even the murderer might already be wise.

But no, that wasn't the point. If she knuckled under

now and let Longdong pimp her for information, that'd be just the opening wedge. From then on, once she let him dominate her by rule of fear—from that moment she'd have him on her back. He'd soon be pimping her for more than information, the shit-ugly sonofabitch. In days or weeks or months, he might even have her on the streets.

"I asked you something, bitch. Is you ready to lay the truth on me—or is you freaking for more coathanger?"

"Fuck you in the teeth, horsecock."

Whoosh! . . . Whooosh! . . . Whoosh!...... Oh, Lord Jesus. The pain was so scorching, tears sprang to her eyes.

Longdong moved to the side of the bed. With walloping underarm swings, he laid his pimp sticks across her bareass. . . . *Whooosh! . . . Whooosh! . . .* Angie wanted to scream in agony.

Suddenly he stopped and turned away, tucking the sticks under his arm. He seemed to be admiring the Matisse tapestry on the wall, that had cost him $90,000 at Parke-Bernet. As if he'd lost all interest in his naked victim lashed to the four-poster.

Bullshit. The ploy didn't fool Angie. It was all a carefully calculated part of his gorilla-mack, ho-taming technique.

It was also the chance she'd been waiting for. Earlier, when he was snorting cocaine, he'd only been making out like he was paying her no mind. But he'd have peeped any false move quick enough.

Now, with his back turned, it was different. Now Angie would find out if her black opal ring was worth all that bread she'd paid for it—and she wasn't talking about the opal itself. The money had gone to a little wizened-up Goldberg in a watch repair on Eighth Avenue, who'd learned his precision trade the hard way as apprentice and journeyman watchmaker in pre-Hitler Germany. He'd designed the spring-loaded mechanism from a mere few sentences' description by Angie.

She pressed her thumb to a trigger inside the ring circlet. Instantly the slender, oval-shaped stone—a good inch and a half long—sprang upright from its setting. And from the top of the stone, an inch-and-a-half metal prong shot out, like a tiny switchblade. It was honed razor-sharp from the finest surgical steel, and its tip now projected a good three inches from the back of her finger.

Curving her hand backward, Angie sawed away frantically at the rope that lashed her wrist to the bed leg. The blade cut through the strands like butter.

But sonofabitch! That motherfuckin' dog was turning around—and now he could see what had happened! Angie's free hand grabbed a bronze African idol from its niche near the bed. She hurled it like a war club and laid Longdong's shaven skull as wide open as a split melon.

The Abominable Cunt Man collapsed in a gory heap—like curled-up dogshit from a Great Dane with bleeding piles, thought Angie with savage glee. She was already slashing at the ropes that held her other limbs.

Both arms free. Now the legs—

Angie leaped off the bed just as Leroy came in the door. Evidently he had heard the thump when his boss collapsed, so he was checking to make sure everything was cool. Angie had the Cobra .38 out of Longdong's boot at the same time Leroy's piece cleared leather.

But Angie was the hotter shot. She put two holes in his chest before Leroy's bullet even plowed into the bed mattress. His body slammed backward under the impact of the double slugs, dumping Snake Man, who was right behind him in the doorway.

Snake Man didn't even try to draw his Tokarev. He

knew the Dark Angel was too fuckin' fast to mess with. He just kicked Leroy's corpse at her—and launched himself off the deck with a spring. The corpse knocked the gun out of Angie's hand. Snake Man threw a round-house right. Angie slipped the punch and slashed him in the face with her switchblade ring—widening his mouth a good two inches. Snake Man screamed and fell back. Angie kicked his head quiet and retrieved the Cobra.

As far as she knew, there was no one else in Long-dong's pad. But any occupants of the flats close by would sure as hell have heard the shots—not to mention Snake Man's bloodcurdling shriek.

She got her shoes, snatched up her dress and hauled ass out the window and down the fire escape. It dropped her into a pitch-dark alley. She slipped on the dress while she glanced around to get her bearings. At the far end of the alley were the back doors of buildings that fronted on West 145th. Angie ran in that direction.

The lights and raucous music from the rear of one establishment indicated a juke joint or bar. Just as she approached, the back door opened and a finger-snapping, nick-nackin dude came out—apparently to take a leak, as if the inside can was full up. He paused in the act of unzipping himself as he spotted Angie, and his eyes lit up like a pinball machine on TILT.

"Hey, pretty girl! You just what I'm looking for! And here you come, right into my arms!"

Angie was suddenly aware that her torn dress left her tits and pussy more or less on full public display. And the dude was coming at her, grabbing for a handful of each. She aikido-twirled and sent him sailing over her shoulder—headfirst into a cinder block wall on her right.

The dude lay still, but his breathing was regular.

The door he'd come out of was still partly open. Enough light filtered out to see by. She for damn sure couldn't go into the juke joint without causing a near riot—but adjoining it was a steel door that looked worth a try.

She frisked the dude and came up with a nail file and a fake pearl stickpin. They should do the trick. In a couple of minutes she'd picked the lock and had the steel door wide open.

Inside was a narrow, gloomy corridor leading to what looked like a dimly lit vestibule and a flight of stairs at the front end. Suddenly Angie clued in. This must be the downstairs hallway of the upper-story flats above the juke joint and whatever establishments adjoined it. And damned if she hadn't hit the jackpot! On the wall near the foot of the stairs was a pay phone!

Angie went back into the alley long enough to fish a handful of coins from the dumped dude's pocket. Her incredible luck held. The fucking phone actually worked! She dialed information and got the number of the Warrick Plaza. But no answer from Jack Bristol's room there after long ringing.

Angie dialed information again, this time got the number of Star Kenning on Park Avenue. A further payment to Ma Bell brought her the snotty voice of a manservant saying:

"This is the Kenning residence."

"I want to speak to Mr. Jack Bristol. It's *extremely* urgent."

"One moment, please. I'll see if he's here."

Finally Jack's voice came on. Jesus, this was break-the-bank night!

"Look, this is Angie," she blurted. "I hate to interrupt anything you may have going there with Star, but I'm in a spot. Can you come and help me?"

"You name it." *What a man!*

Knowing the location of Longdong's crib, Angie was able to give him exact directions.

"Fast as I can," Jack promised.

Angie skulked back into the gloom at the rear of the hallway while she waited. Several people came in or went out. After twenty minutes or so, she heard his code knock. Angie rushed to open the door. And melted into his arms.

"Oh, man! Do you ever look good to me!"

"Sweetie, you not only look good, you feel good!" said Jack. Star's Rolls had sped him to the parking garage on East 50th, where he'd gotten out the Firebird and gunned his way north to Angie's rescue.

Her ass was too painful to sit on, but Jack managed to get her ensconced on her side in fair comfort with her legs curled up.

"Where to?" he said as they took off.

The doorman would still be on duty at the Turtle Bay Towers, so Angie directed Jack to an underground garage on East 138th Street. Its door horned open, and they drove down a curving ramp to a vast, whitewashed basement room. At one end was a well-equipped automotive service bay, a Jag, a Hornet, a Rolls and a gleaming yellow VW Dasher. The other half of the area comprised a tiny but comfortable living apartment.

"My pied-à-terre," said Angie with a grin. "Otherwise known as the Dark Angel's emergency hidey-hole."

Her backside felt too painful even for the running water of a lukewarm shower. Angie shed what was left of her dress and got a bulbous, unlabeled green bottle out of the lavatory medicine cabinet.

"What's that?" asked Jack.

"Some kind of magic herb liniment. A local Voodoo queen whomps it up in her bathtub. Go ahead and laugh if you like, but the stuff actually works."

She gave Jack the bottle and some cotton batting, then lay face down on the bed. He was unable to resist kissing the wounded area, after which he dabbed it gen-

139

tly with the liniment, while they exchanged slightly censored accounts of their respective evenings' activities.

"So what was Star's story on Laidlaw Pike?" said Angie.

"She says he came to her last October with a heavy-breathing yarn about a strike made by Emerald Oil—which might have been true enough. But Star wasn't all that sure Pike knew where. Her agents confirmed that Pike was down on his luck, so she figured the whole thing was probably just a pitch to get himself back in business. Hence, she turned him down—or so she says."

"Do you buy her story?" asked Angie delicately.

"Yes, I think so," said Jack after a thoughtful moment. "At least I can't see any reason for her to lie—and it does tie in with her present attempt to buy out Emerald Oil, or at least fish around for data."

"Hmm. Which still leaves open the question of who *did* buy Pike's story and finance his expedition."

"There's still Xerxes Zagrevi and his E-Z Oil Consortium," Jack pointed out.

"True. Very true," said Angie.

"I, uh, take it you had no time tonight to get a line on any phonies *inside* Emerald Oil?"

"Not really. But I'd sure agree Matt Yarrow makes a choice suspect. He's not only a slimy sonofabitch, he's got a very jumpy conscience about *something*—and from what you say, he did have a motive. Your father's death jumped him up to the top brass. Plus which, he was close to all technical data before the murder—and now he's sitting right on top of it." Angie added over her shoulder, "He also seems to be rather tight with that dude you named as Number Two choice—George Quinn, the company treasurer. At least I heard someone calling him George."

"That'd be Quinn. He's the only George in the

140

group." Jack continued applying liniment to her buttocks. "So where do we go from here, Angie?"

"What about this house where your father was killed?"

"It's up on the edge of the Catskills. We passed about twenty miles from it on the way to Lake Nippigong."

"Could you face a visit there?"

Jack shrugged. "Why not?"

"Okay. Let's take a run up there tomorrow. We've played around with motives and the oil business. Maybe it's time to take a look at the physical facts of how and where"

When Jack finished dabbing her backside, Angie got up from the bed. "Speaking of taking a look at the physical facts," she grinned wryly, "my butt isn't the only area in need of medication."

She hoisted one foot up on the bed in order to examine her inflamed pubic region. "Give me the bottle and some cotton."

"I'll do it," said Jack.

It was difficult for him to avoid an erection—a fact not unnoticed by the Dark Angel.

"Honey, I'm too sore for any action right now," Angie murmured. "But like the man says, there's more than one way to skin a cat."

Jack blushed and shook his head. "I can wait."

Angie shucked her stockings and Jack undressed and they got in bed and turned off the light and lay in the darkness in each other's arms.

"Hey, I almost forgot!" Angie exclaimed.

"Forgot what?"

"What I was going to ask you on the phone this afternoon, just as you got called away by Madame Star."

"What was that?"

"An entry in Pike's date book. Very recent. But dammit, I can't remember the name."

"What was the nature of the entry?" said Jack.

"An appointment, I guess . . . something urgent."

"You can't remember anything else about it?"

Angie said slowly, "Well, the name was something like Hardy . . . or Underwood."

Jack grinned in the dark. "Those aren't exactly alike."

"Some association probably," mused Angie. "Let's see. Hardy. Hardy. . . . Thomas Hardy, the novelist . . . Oliver Hardy, that's better. . . . And Underwood—well, typewriters. Typewriters. Underwood Olivetti. Hey, there's something! Oliver Hardy, Olivetti . . . *Olivet!* That was it, I'm sure! Olivet." As Angie repeated the name, the date book entry suddenly flashed clearly before her mind's eye.

Olivet. Must make him see potential. Emphasize time factor!

Chapter Fourteen

Angie quoted the date book entry aloud to Jack. But he was unable to offer any explanation.

"You've never heard the name Olivet since you got involved with Emerald Oil?" the Dark Angel asked.

"Not that I recall offhand. But I'll ask around."

By morning, the Voodoo liniment had done its magic. At least most of the soreness was gone from Angie's intimate areas—a happy development which she and Jack proceeded to celebrate in appropriate fashion.

They showered and breakfasted heartily on bacon and eggs and sallied forth in the Firebird.

"If you don't mind, there's a stop I'd like to make first on East 62nd," said Angie.

She found Moira Cane awake and as happy-go-lucky as ever—entirely unconcerned about missing her date the night before, even after Angie confessed to taking her place.

"I could care what that shitheel Longdong thinks about me not showing," Moira shrugged.

"The shitheel's probably not thinking *anything* right now," said Angie. "I left him with his skull wide open and with a head like that nigger's got, they'll probably need a riveting machine to close it."

"You worried about the cops, honey?"

"Hell, no," said Angie. "That's the last thing his stable would want—having the rollers poke their noses into Longdong's affairs. They'll find some way to tidy up and sweep it all under the carpet. Longdong'll lose so much face from what happened last night, he's finished as a boss mack, even if he doesn't wind up on a slab in the morgue. By the time the horse doctors get his head back together, his ladies will probably all have cut loose and chosen other pimps."

Moira put her arms around the Dark Angel. "Let's go back to bed, darling."

Angie giggled. "Just came from there, honey—and I've got a John waiting downstairs. But yesterday was fun. We'll try it again sometime. What I really came for was my alligator shoulder bag."

The Dark Angel went back down to Jack Bristol in the Firebird feeling fully herself again. With her trusty Louisville slugger dangling from her shoulder and the pearl-gripped Baby Browning inside, she once more had it all together.

Something less than two hours later, the Firebird turned off the New York State Thruway and headed for the town of Vanwycksburg, nestling near the foot of the Catskills.

"Would you like to talk to the cop who handled the investigation into Dad's murder?" Jack asked.

"Good idea," Angie agreed.

Vanwycksburg turned out to be a sprawling little farming community with an up-to-date shopping mall on the outskirts near the highway, and a neat but drowsy downtown area of old-fashioned red brick buildings.

Jack parked in front of the police station adjoining the town hall and they went inside. A uniformed cop behind the raised counter gave them a questioning look, which lingered on Angela Harpe in her white-collared, candy-striped halter dress, hemmed high on supple brown thighs.

"Sergeant Ruhr," said Jack.

The cop picked up a phone. "Got a couple of visitors out here, Sergeant."

Presently they heard a door opening. A stocky officer with thinning sandy hair appeared in the archway at the left of the counter. He had sergeant's stripes on his arm, and a big knurl-gripped Colt holstered on his hip.

"I don't know if you remember me or not, Sergeant. I'm Jack Bristol."

"Yeah, I remember you." A brief perfunctory handshake.

"Could we speak to you a few minutes?"

"Okay." Ruhr turned and led the way back to his office. "Sit down." He gestured them to a couple of chairs and started to deposit himself behind a battered desk.

Jack remained standing. "I don't know if you've ever heard of the Dark Angel——"

"I've heard of her."

"This is she. Miss Angela Harpe. Sergeant Ruhr." Ruhr nodded. "Hiya."

Angie just looked at him. "Like to see my license as a private detective?"

"Well, yeah. Now that you mention it, I guess maybe I would."

She showed him, and they finally sat down.

"What can I do for you?" said Sergeant Ruhr with all the interested warmth of a Manhattan subway window cashier confronted by a customer with a question.

"Any new developments on my father's murder since last fall?" asked Jack.

"Not really. We're still working on it."

"I've retained Miss Harpe to investigate," said Jack, "in the hope she may be able to turn up some helpful information. When we leave here, I'll show her Dad's house—but, first, I thought you might give her the basic facts, since you were on the case right from the start."

"What would she like to know?"

"Anything you care to tell me," said Angie.

Sergeant Ruhr shook out a Marlboro and lit it without offering the pack. "Well, he was shot with a .22. The experts up in Albany think the bullet may have come from a target pistol—with a silencer. His body wasn't found till the next morning, when the milkman spotted it through the open window. He was slumped in an easy chair in front of the television set with the thing still going. Medical examiner placed the time of death at somewhere around nine o'clock the previous evening— but that's only a ball-park estimate. Probable trajectory indicates the bullet came through the window, which is confirmed by a hole in the screen. The entrance wound was right between the eyes, but assuming his attention was on the TV, he probably had no glimpse or warning of the killer—especially since it was dark outside."

Angie asked, "Did you draw any other conclusions from the circumstances of the murder?"

Ruhr settled back and scratched his chin with the thumbnail of his cigarette hand. "Oh, maybe one or two. The neatness of the killing suggests an expert job, maybe by a hired hit man. On the other hand, you might argue, how did the killer know he'd find Mr. Bristol there at the TV set, with a clear line of fire from the window? That is, unless someone had instructed him in the victim's habits. Which in turn suggests maybe the hit man was hired by a close personal friend."

Angie said, "You mean some friend who had visited him *here* frequently and knew the setup."

Sergeant Ruhr nodded silently and drew on his cigarette.

"I assume you've questioned the neighbors about visitors?"

"Tried to. Not much luck. His house is all alone, up on a knoll or hillside, with a lot of trees, so he has no neighbors who can really see much. On top of which, people around here make a habit of minding their own business. Pretty good habit, we think."

"Not where murder's concerned, I hope," said Angie coolly. "Have you turned up any leads at all?"

"One—if you can call it a lead. He was killed on Halloween. A couple of kids who were out trick-or-treating that night claim they saw a van parked near the foot of the hill—and someone going up the path toward Bristol's house."

"What did this 'someone' look like?"

"Dark hat, long dark coat and a skull head—with big round eyes."

Angie frowned. "A *skull head?*"

"It was Halloween, remember? Could be the killer played cute and wore a mask."

"You said a skull head, not a skull face."

Sergeant Ruhr shrugged irritably. "All right, so maybe it was one of these rubber jobs that you pull over your whole head, and not just a face mask. . . . That's assuming the kids didn't just imagine the whole thing in the first place."

"I see," said Angie. "Anything else you can give me?"

"No, Miss Harpe. I would say that's about all."

"We needn't keep you, then. Thanks for the information."

Jack's face looked annoyed as the Firebird pulled away from the police station. "Sorry about that, Angie. . . . I don't know what the heck was wrong with *him* today."

"Wagner Axby probably—among other things."

"For Pete's sake." Jack threw her a startled glance. "I never even thought of that."

147

"If he can reach a detective lieutenant in New York City, there's no reason why he can't reach a sergeant up here in Vanwycksburg. Not that it matters a fiddler's fuck." She grinned and gave Jack's arm a reassuring squeeze.

The town was pure Norman Rockwell, straight out of the *Saturday Evening Post*. Old-fashioned houses with verandas, flowerbeds, white picket fences. Quiet, tree-shaded streets.

"How did your father happen to locate up here?" asked Angela Harpe.

"He was born and raised in Kingston. I guess he always liked the area. Mostly it was just a place to rest up and get away from it all—what the land sharks call a 'leisure home.' Actually Dad's real home base was a condominium down in Houston."

The houses were strung farther apart toward the outskirts of town, and the paved street became a dirt road. Finally Jack turned up a rutted cinder drive. It led steeply up a hillside, scattered with maples and poplars, to Lang Bristol's white frame bungalow.

They got out of the car and approached the house on foot. There was a low hedge enclosing a yard, some untended rose bushes and a garage adjoining the house. The window screening was rusted from having been left on all winter.

"What do you suppose your dad did with himself up here?" Angie asked curiously. "How would he pass the time?"

"Oh, reading, sleeping, drinking beer, watching TV. I gather he went out tramping in the woods almost every day. Actually, I doubt if he was ever here more than a week at a time. Then he'd drive down to New York for one of his binges."

"He had a car?"

"Yeah, a British Rover. I had the executor sell it,

since I was going down to Houston and then South America."

"But you kept the house."

Jack nodded. "Yeah. Somehow I felt I shouldn't sell it till the murder was solved. Just in case it might hold a clue."

He pointed out the bullet hole in the screen. With a key on his ring, he unlocked the front door and they went inside. The air was musty and stale. In the front parlor Angie saw a leather reclining chair facing a Zenith 19-inch color TV.

"That's where his body was found?"

"Yeah."

Angie wandered around, trying to get the intangible feel of the house and the person who had lived and died there. "Did someone go through his correspondence and personal effects?"

"I did," said Jack. "There wasn't anything much. Practically all his personal papers and legal documents were at the condominium in Texas."

The bedroom was monastic in its simplicity. Angie glanced through the dresser drawers, then opened the old-fashioned wardrobe. Something caught her eye. It was the buckle on a belt looped around one of the pairs of hangered trousers.

Angie bent to examine it. The buckle was a kind seldom seen anymore, having a slip fastener rather than a prong and holes. But it was the insignia on the buckle which had roused her interest—the familiar Emerald Oil green shamrock trademark with the letter E in the center. Each of the three shamrock leaves was set with a glittering green stone.

Angie pulled the belt out of the trouser loops and took it over to the window for a closer scrutiny.

"Do you know where your dad got this, Jack?"

"Probably a company award, I should think. You

149

know——one of those 'twenty-five years of faithful service' things. Tell you the truth, I only looked in that wardrobe once and never even noticed it. I suppose it's probably valuable, if those stones are real emeralds."

Angie nodded. "May I take this along with us? I don't mean to keep it, of course."

"Sure. . . . Got something in mind?"

"Maybe." As she spoke, Angie was unsnapping the leather belt so as to remove the buckle. "Since we've come this far, could we take another run up to Lake Nippigong and see Fergus Doyle again?"

"Fine with me," said Jack. "We can go have lunch somewhere and give him a call from the restaurant."

As they were leaving the house and locking up, Angie murmured, "Oh, oh. We're under surveillance."

"What do you mean?"

"Take a gander down the hill."

A white and green police car was parked near the foot of the cinder drive.

"That sonofabitch!" muttered Jack, forgetting momentarily that he was in the presence of a lady.

"Let me back inside for a minute," said Angie.

Jack unlocked the door. She came out again presently, holding some folded white paper toweling from the kitchen.

When the Firebird came down the cinder drive into the dirt road, Angie asked Jack to pull up alongside the police car. Sergeant Ruhr was seated at the wheel, smoking. He stared back at them with an expression of bland insolence.

"Sergeant," said Angie out the window.

"Yes, ma'am?"

"This house being unoccupied and all, do you keep it under pretty good observation?"

"We try to."

"Swell. Then probably there'll be no more signs chalked up."

"Signs? What do you mean?"

"Somebody's written something rather offensive up there."

Sergeant Ruhr frowned suspiciously at the Dark Angel. "Oh, yeah? What've they written?"

Angie unrolled the paper toweling and held it up to the window. Lettered in red marker pen were the words:

FUCK YOU

The sergeant's face turned as red as the letters, but his blurted obscenity was lost as Jack pulled away.

They lunched at a roadside restaurant on something called "char-broiled steerburgers 'n fries." The coffee, at least, was good enough for seconds. Stirring in a packet of sugar, Angie asked, "Jack, what was your mother's name?"

"Millicent Clara Lowell Bristol. Why?"

The Dark Angel shrugged evasively. "Just a crazy idea I'm toying with. Do you know the specific grounds for her divorce from your father?"

"Not exactly. I assume it was his being away from home so much, plus his drink and—well, his general refusal to be domesticated."

"Mmm. . . . There's a phone booth over there. Why don't you make that call to Fergus Doyle while I go tease my hair."

Doyle seemed genuinely delighted at the prospect of seeing them again. When they arrived an hour later, he suggested they chat in the summerhouse.

"It's quite delightful at this time of the afternoon."

A drowsy air of warmth hung over the lake and

grounds, filled with the buzzing of insects and muted quacking from the marshes. The summerhouse was an elaborate octagonal structure with a wood-louvred door and sides that were mostly glass-jalousied windows. The huge, fright-faced manservant Nemo drew drapes along the house side to shut out the hotly slanting afternoon sun, and then brought them drinks.

"Useful chap, Nemo," murmured Doyle. "I hardly know what I'd do without him."

"How long has he been with you?" asked Angie.

"Oh, let me see. I gave him a job as an oil field roustabout when I first learned about his case. But he and his wife have been more or less part of the family since 1960." Doyle smiled. "However, I mustn't bore you. I gather you two came here with something on your minds."

Angie returned his smile and nodded. "No use pretending it's a purely social call, Fergus—though on a day like this, I wish it were."

She started to open her shoulder bag, then paused and glanced at Jack Bristol. "Jack, forgive my asking him this. Fergus, do you know what broke up Lang Bristol's marriage?"

The old man's gaze shifted uncomfortably. "In a general way, I suppose I do."

"Be as specific as you can, please. Skip the drinking and what we know about."

There was a brief silence before Doyle replied, "In those days, Lang was quite a ladies' man. He couldn't keep away from women, and they couldn't keep away from him. Eventually his wife, Jack's mother, refused to put up with it any longer."

Angie said, "Was there any particular woman?"

"I believe there may have been. I didn't pry."

Angie fished the belt buckle with the green shamrock insigne out of her bag. "Is this a company award?"

152

Fergus Doyle examined it with lively interest. "Good Lord, no. Where did you get this?"

"Off a belt belonging to Lang Bristol."

Doyle shook his head, frowning curiously. "Odd I never recall seeing him wear it. Emerald Oil has always tried to recognize and reward faithful service—but I'm afraid the company's never been wealthy enough to hand out this sort of thing. Assuming, of course, that these stones are real emeralds. And I rather think they are."

"So do I," said Angie. "Which made me wonder. Can you see those letters engraved in each corner of the buckle, between the leaves and stem of the shamrock? They're rather worn down but you can still make them out if you hold it up to the light."

"Ah, yes. . . . E, S, M, E."

"May I see?" said Jack, getting up from his chair.

"Any idea what those letters stand for?" asked Angie.

"I'm afraid not," said Doyle. "Of course, the Spanish word for emerald is *esmeralda*. So I suppose they could be the first four letters of the company name—in Spanish."

"Esme is also a *woman's* name," said the Dark Angel.

"So it is," said Doyle.

Jack glanced at Angie. "You think some old flame may have given this to Dad?"

"Maybe. A buckle like that with gemstones set in shiny silver metal is certainly an eyecatcher. Yet neither you nor Fergus ever recalls seeing it—which suggests your father was careful to wear it only at certain times, probably with a suitcoat or vest so it wouldn't be noticed." She took the buckle from Jack and replaced it in her shoulder bag. "Anyhow, it's an intriguing little mystery. But we've another question to ask you, Fergus."

"Ask away, my dear."

"Does the name 'Olivet' mean anything to you?"

"Of course. Frank Olivet. He's a very old and dear friend."

"Who is he aside from that?"

"Well, I would describe him as a self-taught engineering genius. He's very well known in the oil industry. Holds patents on a number of technical devices—instruments, gauges, that sort of thing—that are used both in drilling and prospecting." Doyle flashed the Dark Angel a curious glance. "May one ask how his name came up in your investigation?"

Angie dimpled. "Let's just say we saw it somewhere we weren't supposed to be looking. Is Olivet located in New York?"

"Yes, he has an office in town, and some sort of lab and workshop where he develops his gimmicks over in New Jersey—near Norwood."

As he finished speaking, Angie stood up suddenly, took two quick steps, and yanked open the louvred wooden door of the summerhouse. Nemo was standing just outside. The expression that passed over his ravaged face was terrible to see. Jack felt slightly sick to his stomach.

To break the embarrassed silence, the Dark Angel said gently, "We must be going, Fergus."

"No, no, no! Surely you'll stay and give us the pleasure of your company at dinner?"

"Thank you. I wish we could, truly, but Jack and I are both anxious to get on with our investigation."

As they drove away, Jack murmured, "Good God! Talk about embarrassing moments. . . . How long do you suppose Nemo was standing there?"

"Quite a while, I suspect." Angie added thoughtfully, "I wonder what his wife's name is?"

Chapter Fifteen

It was nearing 4:30 as they headed toward the Thruway.

"Let's find a phone and try to reach Olivet," Angie suggested. "With luck, we might be able to see him this evening."

She made the call from an Exxon station. A man's voice answered.

Angie said, "Frank Olivet?"

"Speaking."

"Mr. Olivet, I'm a private detective. Perhaps you've heard of the Dark Angel?"

There was a pause, a dry chuckle. "Of course. Who hasn't. I hope you're not pulling my leg."

"Far from it. I'm calling in connection with a murder case. I've been retained by a Mr. Jack Bristol to investigate the death of his father, an oil man named Lang Bristol."

She could almost hear his catch of breath. "I see."

"You knew Lang Bristol?"

"Yes. Very well."

"Mr. Olivet, I hate to ask a favor when you don't even know me. Ordinarily I wouldn't bother you after office hours, but—"

"Don't worry about that. I don't keep rigid hours. My office and apartment are in the same place."

"Then—would it be possible to see you this evening?"

"What's the matter with right now?" said Olivet.

"Unfortunately," said Angie, "we're quite a ways upstate at this moment. I'm calling from a gas station."

"How long would it take you to get here?"

"Oh, maybe three hours."

Olivet hesitated. "Well, I'm due at a dinner party this evening, but if you can be here by seven-thirty, I'll give you half an hour."

"Thank you, Mr. Olivet. We'll make it."

His apartment-cum-office turned out to be a penthouse overlooking Central Park. A white-jacketed Japanese houseman admitted them to a luxurious sitting room with tasteful modern furniture and a colorful De Kooning canvas in red, green and black displayed to excellent advantage on one wall.

Frank Olivet himself was a tall, spare man with silvering dark hair. About fifty, Angie decided. Rather good-looking.

"We can go into my office, if you prefer," he said as they shook hands, "but I thought we'd be more comfortable in here. What would you like to drink?"

"It's good of you to see us at all, sir. We don't want to take up any unnecessary time—"

"Nonsense. Will martinis do?"

"I'd love one," said Angie. Jack went along.

The houseman brought their drinks on a tray with amazing promptness and poured out three glasses from a frosted shaker.

"As I told this young lady on the phone, I knew your father, Jack," said Olivet. "May I call you Jack?"

"Please do."

"It's rather late to be offering condolences, but I'm.

sure he's missed by many people. He was a good man, your father. A man with a lot of friends." Olivet spoke somberly, as if he meant what he was saying, and not just offering platitudes.

"Thank you, sir," said Jack. "I'll be grateful if you can answer Miss Harpe's questions."

"A question of my own first, if I may. How did you get my name?"

"Actually, we had *only* the name Olivet to begin with," said Angie. "It was Fergus Doyle who identified you as Frank Olivet and told us your line of business."

Olivet smiled. "The screwball kid inventor?"

"As a matter of fact, he called you an engineering genius."

"That's typically kind of Fergus. I don't suppose he mentioned how much I owe him personally."

"No, he just described you as a very old and dear friend," said Angie.

Olivet acknowledged the description with a nod. "The truth is, if it weren't for Fergus, I'd probably still be repairing slot machines for the New York-New Jersey mobs. That was my original line of work."

Jack said, "You mean Mr. Doyle got you into oil field engineering?"

"He did more than that—he put me in business. You see, I grew up on the Lower East Side. No education, a dropout actually—just a kid with a certain mechanical knack. Then one day I happened to read a technical article on oil drilling. It got me interested. I started thinking and worked out an idea on how to improve the rotating cones used on certain types of drill bits. I didn't know what the hell to do with my idea, but I just happened to see Fergus Doyle's name in the paper, so I barged into his office one morning and showed him my designs."

"I take it he liked your idea," said Angie.

Olivet gave a reminiscent chuckle. "He told me somebody had already *had* the same idea. But darned if he didn't take an interest in this little guinea nobody. He encouraged me to go to night classes, and lent me money from time to time. Finally he financed production of my first successful invention—a type of control valve used on oil well 'Christmas trees'—and helped me get it on the market."

Angie murmured, "Sounds like a father-son relationship."

"That's a pretty fair description, Miss Harpe. But we're getting away from the point of your visit. How can I help you?"

"A minute ago you asked how we got your name. May I ask you to keep a trade secret?"

"I sure as hell wouldn't have lasted long in the oil industry if I couldn't do that."

"Thanks. We happened to see your name jotted down in an appointment book belonging to Laidlaw Pike."

A slightly startled grin appeared on Olivet's face. "Well, I'll be damned."

"The exact entry, as I recall it," Angie went on, "reads: *Olivet. Must make him see potential. Emphasize time factor.*"

"Hmm, interesting—but about what I would expect," said Olivet. "He's already phoned for an appointment."

"Any idea what he wants to see you about?"

"Wouldn't say over the phone, but it's not hard to guess. I should imagine he wants me to invest in this new wildcatting venture of his down in South America."

Angie regarded the engineer thoughtfully. "I see."

"You both look a bit disappointed," said Olivet.

"We've no reason to be," said Jack politely, "after you've been kind enough to see us on such short notice."

"May one ask how Pike's appointment with me relates to your father's murder?"

158

Jack glanced at Angie. She hesitated, choosing her words carefully. "As you can probably guess, Mr. Olivet, we haven't much to go on at this late date. But we think Lang Bristol's murder may be connected with his last prospecting expedition down in Colombia. We also think that that original expedition—well, shall we say, *inspired* Pike's present venture in the same area. But there are a couple of odd things we don't understand about the . . . the whole picture in that part of Colombia just now. I guess we were hoping you might be able to shed some light."

"I think I understand, Miss Harpe. Perhaps I'll know more after I've talked to him."

"Thanks. If anything occurs to you that might bear on our investigation, we'll appreciate it if you'll get in touch with one of us. Jack's at the Warrick Plaza, and this number will reach me most any time." Angie handed him a card from her bag.

"I'll do that, Miss Harpe. It's been interesting meeting the famous Dark Angel. And, Jack, it's good meeting your father's son."

It was much later when Angela Harpe returned alone to her pad. She and Jack had said good night in his car outside the Turtle Bay Towers.

She knew the moment she inserted her key and started to turn it that the lock had been jimmied. But by then it was too late. The door was yanked open and a gun was jammed in her cheek. Another was pointing at her belly.

Her apartment was dark, but the light from the corridor showed her their faces. The dude whose gun muzzle was scraping her cheekbone was the Chigro she had laid out cold on the sidewalk just before her first meeting with Xerxes Zagrevi. The other gunsel, who had pulled open the door, was Creepo—otherwise known as Afro Boy—who had tried to rape her in her office.

159

"Welcome home, bitch!" Afro Boy was grinning.

The Chigro was merely nasty. He grabbed Angie's arm and swung her inside with a force that almost landed her on the floor. "Take her fuckin' bag."

"Good thinking, blood."

They made her lean against the wall. Afro Boy lifted her skirt and playfully jammed the gun up her ass while the Chig was taping her mouth. Then they handcuffed her wrists behind her.

It was all so businesslike Angie knew the job had been planned carefully in advance. Which obviously meant by someone other than these two stupid shits.

Afro Boy was inclined to play a bit, prying inside her panties and down the neck of her dress. But the Chigro grunted impatiently, "Come on! Quit fuckin' around! Let's blow!"

They took her up in the elevator to the roof and out through the penthouse conservatory—the same way Angie had exited on the evening of her summons by Miss Nightgrove to meet Xerxes. Apparently these two apes had entered via the same route, no doubt inspired by her earlier example.

A telescoping magnesium ladder of the kind favored by cat burglars was propped from the roof of the adjoining older building up to the parapet of the Turtle Bay Towers. Afro Boy descended first and fielded Angie as the Chigro lowered her on a line slung under her arms. The rest of the way down was via fire escape.

A big Chrysler Imperial was parked near the outlet of the narrow alleyway. Afro Boy kept Angie out of sight while the Chigro got the trunk open. Then they dumped her in, slammed the lid and took off.

The ride was pure hell in the stuffy, gasoline-fumed trunk compartment, her limbs cramped by the spare tire, her head thumping painfully against the metal trunk floor. At times, with her mouth taped, the Dark Angel seriously feared she might suffocate. But she slowed her breathing, fixed her thoughts on the One, the Indivisible, the All-Encompassing Brahman, and gradually relaxed into a state of semi-samhadic bliss.

Some time later, she felt the car slowing and heard the doors open and slam as the two torpedoes got out. In spite of her yogic trance, a portion of Angie's mind had retained its sense of direction, a consciousness of bridge-crossing and roadbed. Intuitively, she felt they were on Long Island.

The trunk lid opened. She was dragged out and held upright while her legs got back their circulation. Still night. The smell of salt air, a sense of water nearby. North Shore, Angie's instinct told her.

They were in a graveled drive, with the massive bulk of an aging Twenties Era stone mansion looming out of the darkness. Lights showed in several windows.

They were met at the front door by Miss Nightgrove, feline and shapely in a sleek-fitting, rust-colored silk jumpsuit. "Take the slut downstairs," she said with a smile of whole-hearted enjoyment at Angie.

Xerxes Zagrevi was waiting in what looked like a bare-floored games room or small gym. He was ensconced, cigar in hand, in a plumply upholstered leather chair. His balding white head with its hooded eyes, beaky nose and raddled neck protruding from an over-sized collar atop a dark lounge suit gave him the look of an elderly buzzard.

Angie was not reassured to note that the ceiling and walls had been soundproofed with white acoustical tiles.

"How nice to see you again, my dear," he murmured in his creaky old man's voice. "I fear, however, the occasion may not be quite so nice for you." To the Chigro, Xerxes added, "You may remove the tape from her mouth."

On one wall was a display of exotic weaponry—a

medieval star mace, a Zulu knobkerrie, a long ghastly looking Philippine bolo knife, a Saxon war axe, a Turkish yataghan. Also equally fearsome, if less warlike, instruments of man's inhumanity to man, such as a flesh pincers from the Spanish Inquisition, an old Royal Navy cat-o'-nine tails and an *eta-yari* or pariah spear, used for the coup-de-grace at Japanese crucifixions. Clearly the prized collection of some bloody-minded asshole—probably Xerxes Zagrevi himself.

Angie's glance lingered on an accompanying collection of offbeat handguns—especially one with a barrel like a bicycle pump.

"Well, well," she murmured. "Don't tell me that's what fired the crochet needle at me in my office the other day?"

"You're referring, no doubt, to the compressed-air needle gun," said Xerxes. "Yes, quite. Chop-Chop there"—indicating the Chigro with a gesture of his cigar hand—"happened to be playing with it in town that morning and was delighted at the chance to use it, after you spoke so rudely to me on the phone."

"You're aware, I presume, that this other retard with the fake Afro had already tried to rape me that same morning?" As the old man frowned in surprise, Angie added, "No, I can see you *weren't* aware. So I assume your little girl, Miss Nightgrove, sent him—out of pique for what happened the previous evening, just before you and I took our limousine ride."

Xerxes Zagrevi threw a glance of displeasure at the brunette in the rust silk jumpsuit. "Is this true, Sybil?"

"I knew that spade bitch would double-cross you," she explained nervously. "I was only trying to correct her attitude."

"We'll discuss the matter later."

"While you're on the subject," said Angie, "you

162

might also look into her sex life a little more closely. I imagine she's screwing Afro Boy on the side, when she's not changing your diapers."

The Iranian's eyes flashed dangerously. "Perhaps you'd do well to concentrate on your own immediate problem, Miss Harpe," he rasped. "At this moment, I would call it rather grave."

"Really? I'm always delighted to have someone take a sympathetic interest in my problems. What's on tonight's agenda, as you see it?"

"Possibly a hysterectomy without anesthesia, should you persist in provoking me, young woman." Zagrevi paused to draw on his cigar. "Your basic mistake, as Sybil has indicated, was attempting to double-cross me in connection with Laidlaw Pike's oil discovery. I warned you in advance against any attempt to deceive me. The needle was a second warning. You ignored both."

"And how am I supposed to have deceived you?" asked Angie.

"Surely I needn't waste time parsing details for a person of your intelligence, Miss Harpe. Your subsequent moves have not gone unobserved, you know. You have involved yourself in an intimate liaison with one of the Emerald Oil group, young Bristol. In his company, you made a second search of Pike's hotel suite. Quite clearly you're playing a double or triple game—seeking to find the location of the Colombian oil strike for your own advantage."

"And now you think I'll cough up the answer to you."

"I'm quite sure you will, Miss Harpe . . . in due time."

Afro Boy and Chop-Chop the Chigro had peeled off their jackets to prepare for action. Afro Boy was heeled with an underarm holster and Chop-Chop's piece was tucked into his trouser waistband—and both were grinning at her. Grinning in anticipation of the fun to come.

Suddenly Angie was filled with loathing. "I'll make you a deal, Wog," she told Zagrevi.

"Indeed? What sort of deal, Miss Harpe?"

"Turn me loose and you can smell my pants."

Zagrevi's face hardened. He gestured with his cigar to his two thugs.

Chop-Chop flicked a wall switch and two steel cables unreeled from the ceiling, each with a clamp on its end. Afro Boy hooked a choker hold on Angie's neck with his right arm and turned her around, so she could no longer see what Chop-Chop was doing. But she could feel him attaching the clamps to her ankles. After that, he must have moved the wall switch back to reel up the cables again—because her feet were suddenly yanked aloft. Then Afro Boy let go of his arm lock on her neck.

For a moment Angie swung back and forth, legs V-ed, wondering how the hell she'd gotten herself into this fucking mess. Her head was down, with her dress bunched around her tits, and her pantied ass was up, like a goose hung high.

Chapter Sixteen

"Well, Miss Harpe, do you find yourself undergoing any change in attitude? Are you, perhaps, seeing things a trifle differently in this position?"

"Yeah, upside down. Which in your case has to be an improvement, Zagrevi. It's a cinch this jive turkey you call Chop-Chop looks a hell of a lot better with his ass end up."

Xerxes Zagrevi gestured again to his two thugs. "The cricket bats, if you please. I'm afraid the young lady still needs chastening."

Afro Boy whaled her across the butt, sending her swinging like a pendulum toward Chop-Chop, who in turn let her have it across the boobs. It was hard to say which hurt worse. They gave her a couple of more chances to compare and decide before letting her come to rest like a plumb bob.

At Zagrevi's signal, the Chigro raised her head enough to arrest a blackout.

"Well, Miss Harpe?"

"What do you think's going to happen to you when I get out of here, Zagrevi?"

"You mean *if* you get out of here, Miss Harpe."

"All right—if."

"To answer your question—nothing very much, Miss Harpe. Surely you don't think your lawyers and your puny financial resources are any match for my own?" The old man chuckled. "With my degree of wealth, you see, the law is my creature. Even if you found out the location of this house, its ownership could never be traced to me. Officially I'm not even in the country at this moment—and my staff could *prove* it!"

Xerxes Zagrevi threw back his vulturine head and cackled with pure malicious enjoyment.

The slimy sonofabitch, thought Angie. As if, with all his billions, another oil field or two mattered a pinch of owl shit. It wasn't just the oil the old fart wanted. It was the anal-sadistic enjoyment of power and authority over other people, to make up for his lost sexual potency. The ultimate freak-off of having another human being at his utter and absolute mercy—especially a luscious nigger female, to spice his senile come.

And suddenly the Dark Angel knew with chilling certainty that, whether she talked or not, Zagrevi never intended her to leave this house alive.

The knowledge sharpened her wits. It cooled her blood-bloated head and steel-hardened her will to live.

Somehow she had to seize the initiative.

To be utterly convincing, she would have to do more than bargain for her life—she would have to make him believe she was still playing for big money stakes.

He signaled the Chigro to drop her head again.

"What makes you think I'll talk in this position, Zagrevi?"

"Because if you don't, my dear, you'll find it increasingly painful. The next step will be to insert a stiff-bristled test tube brush into your vagina and scrub it back and forth."

"Persuasive up to a point, I'll admit. But I thought you were a man who valued efficiency."

166

"I like to think so, Miss Harpe."

"Then hasn't it occurred to you I might become more cooperative and helpful once you decide to cut me in for a full share of the pot?"

Zagrevi tittered drily. "To be quite honest, my dear, I'm not sure you have any information at all to offer. I'm merely—as you yourself might say—checking out the possibility."

"And if I were to convince you?"

The old man spread his hand. "By all means, feel free to try."

Angie was growing increasingly giddy from hanging upside down. Somehow she had to concentrate, to force the blood back from her overstressed brain by sheer will power. "What do you suppose has happened to all the data from Pike's prospecting expedition—the seismograph records, the stratigraphic charts, the gravity and magnetic determinations?"

"Interesting point, Miss Harpe. I see you've acquired some technical expertise since last we talked. My own guess would be that Pike has the data safely stored outside this country—probably in Colombia or perhaps in Rio or even Mexico. Which makes me all the more certain that he must have brought back some sort of summary map, showing where the oil lies."

"I'm afraid you've overlooked an angle, Zagrevi."

"Such as?"

"What makes you so sure he wasn't sending back all that data regularly—*to another oil company?*"

The effect on Zagrevi was striking. His face darkened. His body stiffened. "Exactly what are you suggesting, Miss Harpe?"

"That you've missed a bet and I've covered it, Zagrevi. Pike's playing a foxier game than even you can imagine—but the oil's still up for grabs. Do you want it or don't you? And how much is it worth in terms of a cut for me?"

She had to talk fast—the room was whirling in front of her eyes. Again Zagrevi signaled Chop-Chop to raise her head.

"What's your proposition, Miss Harpe?"

"Let me down out of here and we'll talk."

"No."

"At least take off these damned handcuffs, so I can ease my own head when I need to."

"No. You've still given me no convincing evidence that you have anything to offer."

"All right, you want proof, I'll give you proof," Angie promised. "Let me make a phone call."

"To whom?"

"Laidlaw Pike."

Zagrevi turned to Miss Nightgrove. "Bring two extension phones and plug them in—one for Miss Harpe and one for me."

When she had done so, Angie told her, "Dial the Hotel Thermidor and hold the phone up to my ear."

The desk clerk's voice answered.

With Chop-Chop supporting her head, Angie spoke into the mouthpiece. "Will you ring Mr. Pike's room, please? Seven-fifteen."

"I'm sorry, the switchboard's closed."

"Please! This is an emergency—it's desperately urgent! I guarantee Mr. Pike will make serious trouble for you tomorrow if you don't ring him!"

The clerk hesitated. "Very well, if you put it that way. But we're not supposed to do this."

Finally another voice came on—an elderly male voice, sleepy and irritable.

"Mr. Pike?" said Angie.

"Speaking. Who is this?"

"Never mind that. I can't identify myself. But this is very important. It relates to your prospecting venture in South America. First of all, I've searched your hotel suite—" . . .

"You've *what?*"

"I've searched your hotel suite twice. And I've turned up some rather interesting information. It happens that someone else is listening in on the phone right now, Mr. Pike, so I'll have to speak in a sort of code. But I think you can understand me. Just listen carefully. *Three green in one red."*

Silence at the other end of the line. A breathy silence.

"I'll repeat that, Mr. Pike," said Angie. *"Three green in one red. . . .* Do you understand what I'm referring to?"

"Yes. . . . Yes, I understand." His voice was tense. "What is it you want?"

"Nothing just now. As I say, someone else is listening in, so I can't talk freely. But you'll hear from me again. Maybe tonight. In case I do, better tell the desk to be sure and put me through. I may have a proposition for you. That's all for now, Mr. Pike."

Angie glanced at Zagrevi—who hung up and gestured Miss Nightgrove to do likewise.

"Well?" said Angie.

The old man's voice was thoughtful, still slightly suspicious. "You're beginning to interest me, Miss Harpe. Conceivably you do have something worthwhile to offer. What exactly is your proposition?"

"Your move next, Zagrevi," Angie retorted. "I've given you a peek at my hand. Now let's see some evidence of good faith on your part. Either let me down or take off these goddamned handcuffs, one or the other. Then I'll say my piece."

Zagrevi paused reluctantly, but finally grunted, "Very well. Undo her wrists."

169

Chop-Chop passed the key to Afro Boy, who proceeded to unlock the cuffs.

Angie chafed her wrists, buying seconds of time to nerve herself. Her heart was thudding. It was now or never. Go for broke.

Slowly, with the supple ease born of her long, hard training in gymnastics, Angie raised her head and shoulders and trunk until she was able to circle her thighs with her arms. She was looking between her legs straight at Afro Boy.

"You cocksucking imitation nigger," she hissed. "How would you like to kiss my ass?"

Afro Boy's face exploded with fury. He lunged at Angie, hands clawing for her throat. She plucked the gun from his holster and shot him point blank in the chest —the bullet blasting upward through his neck and skull.

But the Dark Angel didn't pause to see the messy results—she had flopped upside down again instantly and was firing a warning shot at Chop-Chop, who stood gaping in stupefied disbelief, his hand belatedly reaching for his gun—till the bullet creased his cheek.

"Freeze, you bastard—or the next one'll blow your fucking head off!" she ordered. "That's better. Now hit that switch and let me down."

He wavered an instant, his face sick with fear—then turned obediently toward the wall switch. Angie seized the opportunity to snap off a shot at Zagrevi and Miss Nightgrove, though both had frozen in panic.

Chop-Chop apparently thought the shot was intended to hurry him up. He hurried. He flicked the switch and the cables unreeled with a *whirr!* Angie broke her fall with her free arm and laid another shot close to his ear —just to keep him in the right frame of mind.

"Up against the wall, slant," she told him in a deadly voice. "Just like you made me do back in town."

He obeyed, literally trembling.

Her glance flicked to Zagrevi and Nightgrove. "Okay, wog—get your bony old ass up out of that chair. Now you and your wet nurse get over there and join him. . . . Move, goddammit, or I'll let daylight through you! . . . Same position as the Chig—and I do mean *lean*. Arms out, hands flat. But don't cluster too close together, if you want some friendly advice. There could still be gunplay."

She waited till they got into position.

"Okay, Chop-Chop, we'll do this by the numbers— slow and easy. You can start by lowering your right hand . . . slowly, I said! . . . Now, use your thumb and forefinger like tweezers and pull the gun out of your pants. Repeat—slow and easy. You try any cute moves and there'll be blood and brains all over that wall. . . . Tha–a–at's right. Now, just drop it."

His piece clattered to the floor.

"Shove it away from you with your foot," said the Dark Angel.

The Chigro obeyed.

Trembling a bit herself now as the tension eased, Angie unlatched the clamps from around her ankles, then retrieved one shoe that had fallen off when she was first hoisted upside down.

Slowly she got to her feet . . . still keeping the three backs covered. . . . Jesus Christ, for a while there she hadn't been too sure she'd ever stand upright again. Angela Harpe breathed a silent prayer of thanks.

Stooping down, she fished in Afro Boy's pockets for the handcuff key—ignoring his condition above the shoulders. Then she picked up the handcuffs.

"Turn around, Chop-Chop." She tossed him the cuffs. "Now listen carefully and get this right, stupid, or I'll shoot off an inch of your dick. I want you to hand-

171

cuff yourself to Miss Nightsoil over there—your right wrist to her right wrist, you facing one way, her facing the opposite. Got that?"

"I dig," the Chigro mumbled.

"Then do it."

He did it.

"Any booze in this joint?" asked Angie.

"There's a bar upstairs," said Miss Nightgrove helpfully, no doubt hoping the Dark Angel would get herself plastered and make some fatal mistake.

"Good," said Angie. "You two lead the way. Zagrevi, you dung-faced old buzzard, you follow them. Both hands in the air. And if you fall on your face going upstairs, I'll laugh like hell."

Progress was slow, since the Chigro had to go up backwards, groping for each step.

The bar was located in a sort of Art Deco lounge, out of a 1933 Warner Brothers Vitaphone movie. The liquor, too, was doubtless well-aged. It looked expensive enough, anyhow, and the supply was plentiful.

Angie took a bottle of vodka with her free hand, smashed off the neck and poured three full glasses.

"The idea is to get you all drunk fast," she explained. "Anybody who doesn't approve, speak up. I can shoot you right now, if you prefer. Makes no difference. Actually it'll save me a lot of trouble."

A universal preference for alcohol was expressed.

While the vodka was being worked on, she questioned the Chigro about the location of the house.

"Oyster Bay," he gulped, between swigs.

Angie picked a bottle of Chivas Regal for the next round—but on second thought decided to stick with vodka all the way. Mixing the tipple might bring on vomiting and clear somebody's head.

"Drink up!" she urged, emphasizing her remark by raising the Smith & Wesson in her hand and sighting it at each one in turn. "If we run out of time, I'll have to shoot you anyhow."

They obeyed with earnest alacrity.

Miss Nightgrove passed out first, soon after the third bottle was opened. Neither Chop-Chop nor Xerxes Zagrevi ever did make a clear-cut and definite transition from consciousness to unconsciousness. Both merely sank by stages into a slobbering, glassy-eyed stupor, spilling the booze all over themselves. Gradually their heads lolled.

The Dark Angel examined them carefully, checking the pupils of their eyes and jabbing each one in the ass with a pin. They were out, all right. For a good long spell. But dammit, the night was slipping by. She'd have to hurry.

She stripped Zagrevi and Chop-Chop, then Nightgrove. It turned out the bitch was menstruating. Angie put the brunette's panties and bra on Xerxes Zagrevi. Then she schlepped them, one by one, out to the Chrysler Imperial. Miss Nightgrove she assigned to the trunk, in the hope it might provide what professional educators call a "learning experience." Zagrevi and the Chigro were stuffed in the back seat and covered from view with some draperies from the house.

Some time later, Angie stopped the car on a dark street in Brooklyn and opened the trunk lid. Miss Nightgrove had barfed and drooled on herself a bit, but otherwise was sleeping soundly. Angie removed the brunette's soiled napkin and sanitary belt so as not to discourage any eventual bypassing vagrants, then hauled her out of the trunk and dumped her in a doorway.

The first pearly streaks of dawn were lightening the sky as she crossed the Williamsburg Bridge to Manhattan. She stopped on the Bowery and unloaded her two remaining passengers. Playfully she arranged them in the sixty-nine position.

Apparently Xerxes was troubled by uneasy dreams of financial disaster and sinking supertankers. The way he was babbling and groaning might wake up his partner, Angie concluded. Have to silence the old bastard somehow.

With a sudden stroke of genius, she remembered a suitable gag and got it out of the trunk.

Chapter Seventeen

Back home at the Turtle Bay Towers, Angie relaxed by treating herself to a warm scented bath, then caught a few hours of sleep. But by 9:47 she was awake and dressed again and on the phone.

She was about to play a long shot. Not quite a complete shot in the dark, but long enough. After last night, though, how could she doubt her luck? She called her black financial reporter friend, Scott Hogarth, at *Business World* and found him already at his desk.

"Angie Harpe again, Hogie. Can you give me a hand?"

"Where would you like it?"

"Between the legs. But since electronic miracles haven't gotten that far yet, would you just check something out for me, please? You can probably find it real fast in *Who's Who* or your clipping files or some such."

"For you, anything, Angel."

She told him what she wanted.

Minutes later she phoned Laidlaw Pike at the Hotel Thermidor. "This is the person who called you last night, Mr. Pike."

"Yes, I . . . I recognize your voice."

"I think you'll find it very much to your advantage to

175

see me as soon as possible," Angie told him. "Have you had breakfast yet?"

"Not yet." His own voice sounded old and tired. "I was just about to make myself some coffee when you rang."

"Fine. Start it perking. I'll be right over."

Meeting Laidlaw Pike face to face, seeing his gaunt dewlaps and harried expression, the Dark Angel almost took pity on him enough to offer to make breakfast herself. Then she remembered he was, after all, a slippery fast-talking operator, and her best chance of worming the truth out of him was to kick him hard in the gonads once she got him down.

Actually, it turned out he not only had coffee going, but hot buttered toast, a pecan ring and grape juice. They sat down across the table from each other in the dinette.

"I'm a private detective, Mr. Pike," Angie began. "Some people call me the Dark Angel."

"Ah, yes. I've read about some of your—your exploits."

"About that phone call last night—it was rather melodramatic," said Angie. "Believe it or not, my life was in danger. The purpose of my call was to mislead the person who was listening in."

Laidlaw Pike frowned, his eyes searching Angie's. "What you're telling me sounds rather alarming."

"It isn't meant to be, Mr. Pike. I'm not here to make trouble for you—at least not if I can help it. I just don't want you to start out under any false assumptions—such as thinking I've come to offer you a price on gemstones or anything like that."

"You said you'd searched my hotel suite. Twice."

Angie nodded. "Yes, that part's true enough—though, of course, I'd deny it officially. The first time was a mistake—someone misled me. The second time

176

was intentional, in connection with a case I'm investigating. That's when I took a closer look at your red-haired playmate and her emerald ovaries."

Pike winced and stared into his coffee cup.

"Actually," Angie went on, "I'm more interested in certain small items I noticed the *first* time I was here. As I recall, you have a nail file and a soap dish and a leather travel case for toilet articles—all bearing the initials E. T. P."

"They were my late wife's initials," said Pike.

"I know," said Angie. "Her name was Esme Tavistock Pike. I checked that out before I came here."

"This is all damned curious, I must say. Do you mind telling me what you're leading up to?"

"In due time, Mr. Pike—don't get impatient. Let me repeat that I'm not here to make trouble."

"Then why *are* you here?"

"For information."

"Ah, I see. A blackmail ploy, no doubt—in hopes of getting in on the ground floor of my oil strike."

"Wrong," said Angie. "Personally, I don't give a damn whether you found oil or not. All I want to know is who financed your prospecting expedition to Colombia—and why."

Pike paused in the act of biting into a piece of toast —genuinely startled. And wary. His voice took on a harder, more aggressive note. "What makes you think anyone financed me? Apparently you didn't check me out quite thoroughly enough, young lady. I'm a wildcatter. I've operated independently for years."

"Come off it, Pike. You can save that kind of horseshit for your public interviews. I happen to know you shoplifted your original lead from an Emerald Oil Company geologist named Lang Bristol. I also know you had no capital of your own to follow up that lead. So you tried to peddle the tip to at least two buyers. Staroleum turned you down. So did E-Z Oil apparently, because Xerxes Zagrevi is now kicking himself in the ass for fear he missed out on a juicy deal—and he's the kind of egomaniac who can't live with that kind of a mistake. But getting back to you, Pike—you finally did take a prospecting team down to Colombia. So obviously someone eventually came up with the bread. Who was it?"

Pike hesitated uncertainly—staring at Angela Harpe and breathing a trifle harder than before. "Let us assume for the sake of argument that what you say is correct. Why should I give you any information, Miss Angel—or whatever your name is?"

"A fair question, Mr. Pike." Angela poured herself some more grape juice. "To begin with, I'm investigating a murder . . ."

"A *murder?*" Pike's eyes widened.

"Yes, the murder of that geologist I just mentioned, Lang Bristol. You and he were long-time acquaintances —if not exactly friends. Mind you, I don't say you killed him. I doubt if there was enough emotional passion left in either of you to generate a killing. But the fact is, Mr. Pike, I could pin Bristol's murder on *you.*"

Pike blurted, "What the devil are you talking about!"

"Well, I suppose you could say two things—two motives," Angie replied coolly. "If I were a D.A., I'd probably put it this way to a grand jury. One—you had elicited inside information from Bristol about a new oil field just discovered by the company he worked for. Then you turned around behind his back and tried to sell that information to a couple of rival outfits. Two—you found out Bristol had once carried on a passionate but adulterous love affair with your wife."

"Damn you! Keep Esme out of this!" Pike exploded.

"I'm explaining how I could pin Lang Bristol's murder on you, Mr. Pike. You asked me. I'm answering."

Angie reached into her shoulder bag and took out the belt buckle with the jeweled shamrock insigne. "Your wife gave this to Bristol, I believe. Her name is engraved on it."

Pike looked old and sick. Finally he nodded slowly. "Yes. She and Bristol had an affair. I knew about it at the time. I've never seen that buckle before, but no doubt you're right. She may well have given it to him."

"Odd sort of gift," mused Angie. "She sounds like a bit of a bitch, if you'll forgive my saying so. From the looks of these, it's as if she were slyly flaunting the affair—daring you and the world to find out. The E stands for Emerald, also Esme—but that's not enough. She had her name actually engraved on the buckle, one letter in each corner—not so noticeable, but still there to be seen if anyone looked closely."

Pike shrugged. "How can I blame her? How can I blame either one of them? Esme was a good enough wife in her own way. And I'm afraid I was never exactly a great lover. Anyhow, it all happened a long time ago. And now it's over and done with. Why rake up the past?"

"No reason, as far as I'm concerned," said Angie. "I told you at the start I'm not here to make trouble. But the fact remains—I could lay out quite a case for the cops right now. To wit. Bristol had given you certain oil strike information in confidence. You betrayed his trust by trying to sell that information. Bristol found out and threatened to get even. A violent argument developed, old passions were stirred up. You were afraid of what he might do—and you'd never forgiven or forgotten the fact that he stole your wife's love. So you decided to kill him."

Pike looked badly shaken. "That's not true! You're twisting a few facts—and making up the rest!"

"Sure I am," said Angie. "I don't buy it myself.

That's why I'm asking you to point me in a new direction."

"By telling you who financed my Colombian oil prospect—"

"And why."

"Damn it," Pike squirmed, "what's that possibly got to do with Lang Bristol's murder?"

"You want to help me find out? Or would you prefer I go to the police with the obvious theory—implicating you?"

Pike sighed heavily and ran his fingers through his thinning hair. "All right. You've made your point. . . . The money for my expedition came from Wagner Axby of Emerald Oil—*at his own suggestion.*"

Angie gasped—the name had come at her so suddenly out of left field. That horse's ass, Wagner Axby! And even more startling—Emerald Oil! "That's quite a stunner, Mr. Pike. And a little hard to believe, if you don't mind my saying so. Why would the president of Emerald Oil pull a stunt like that?

"I don't look gift horses in the mouth, Miss Angel. . . . I can guess, of course."

"Go ahead and guess."

"Emerald was in bad shape. But rumors spread that they were zeroing in on a new oil field. I assume Axby heard those rumors and decided to make hay while the sun was shining."

"By creating the impression that an oil rush was on, down in Colombia."

Pike nodded. "Exactly. Emerald itself was sending out another team—and if I went along with his proposition, I'd be heading up a venture in the same area. It creates a climate of belief, so to speak. A stroke of management genius on Axby's part, let's face it. Suddenly Emerald Oil begins to look like a red-hot property. . . . And Staroleum, it now appears, has taken the bait."

Angie's face wore a puzzled frown. "Just one thing I don't understand. All this doesn't jibe with Lang Bristol's tip. You admit he did tell you Emerald was close to a new oil discovery?"

"Even more definite than that. Lang was a bit drunk at the time, of course, but he let slip that Emerald had a strike."

"Yet the company president comes to you soon afterward and offers to stake you to a prospect in the same area—thereby practically admitting the whole thing's a load of hot con."

Pike shrugged again. "That's about the size of it."

"While we're on the subject," said Angie, "I take it those original rumors stemmed from your own attempts to peddle Bristol's tip to Staroleum and E-Z Oil?"

"Probably. Gossip and leaks travel fast in the oil industry."

"I'm fascinated to know what you'd have used for hard facts, if either company had bought your deal. You really had nothing to go on but Bristol's tip, did you?"

"True. But I know Colombia, you see. From various remarks Lang dropped, it wasn't hard to pinpoint the area where he'd been prospecting. I was prepared to put up a plausible smoke screen."

Angie smiled. "You're a con man, Mr. Pike."

He smiled back wearily. "I've been an oil wildcatter most of my adult life, Miss Angel. One learns to—shall we say, cope with such problems along the way."

For a moment Angie was reminded poignantly of Fergus Doyle's metaphor about old desert rats searching endlessly for gold, knowing they'll never find it. She switched her attention back to the problem at hand. "The harsh fact which still comes through is that Axby apparently had no faith in his own chief geologist. . . . Did he leave it entirely up to you where you'd prospect in Colombia?"

"Oh, no," Pike corrected her sharply. "By no means. Axby's a hard man with a dollar. As long as Emerald was going to stake my expedition, he figured the money might as well be spent as usefully as possible. He laid out certain specific terrain he wanted me to prospect—and of course I contributed a few ideas of my own."

"And the arrangement was, you'd feed the data back to Emerald?"

"Right. For a guaranteed ten percent share in any leases they might purchase and develop, based on my survey."

Angie said, "But you found no oil?"

"None."

"Actually, of course, you still can't be sure whether or not Emerald itself has found oil."

"No. Literally speaking, I suppose that's true."

"But you doubt it?"

Pike smiled thinly. "Let's say I'm no novice in this racket."

"Okay, point taken," said Angie. "One more question while we're face to face, Mr. Pike. Am I right in assuming there's some connection between Frank Olivet and what you're hiding in that trunk?"

From the look on his face, Pike was plainly startled. "As a matter of fact, there is," he admitted grudgingly, "though I can't imagine how you guessed it. He certainly never advertised the fact. Olivet designed and built that robot for me back in '62. Cost me $25,000. I was flush from the sale of a couple of Canadian leases—and Frank was still on his way up in the oil business—anxious to cater to a customer's fancy, you might say. We were drinking one day down in Tulsa and—well, the idea took shape."

"Interesting," said Angie with a smile. "Actually that's not quite what I meant. I was referring to your three raw emeralds—not their fur-trimmed jewel box."

Pike hastily readjusted his sights. "My emeralds? . . . What about them?" he asked suspiciously.

"Relax," said Angie. "I'm not about to broadcast your little secret. But it's not all that hard to clue in on, either. I mean, you've got some raw emeralds—emeralds are found in Colombia—and you've just been down there on an oil prospect. Ergo, you may not have found oil for Axby, but it looks like you're hot on the trail of an emerald mine for Laidlaw Pike."

"You're a shrewd young woman, Miss Angel."

"I think I may as well bare all and tell you my name's Harpe, Mr. Pike—Angela Harpe. And I happen to know you've got an appointment with Frank Olivet. Is it safe to assume you want to see him about those gemstones?"

Pike nodded. "Quite correct. Like any other enterprise, it takes capital to develop an emerald mine. I'm hoping I can persuade him to invest." A sudden glint of interest kindled in Pike's deep-set eyes. "You're said to be very successful in your profession, Miss Harpe—and I gather you work for large fees. I don't suppose *you* would be interested in such an undertaking?"

Angie finished her coffee and, with a smile, rose to leave. "I may live dangerously, Mr. Pike—but when it comes to salting away my hard-earned money, I'm afraid I prefer safer, more humdrum investments than emerald mines."

The Dark Angel came out of the Hotel Thermidor into the May sunshine, thoughtfully humming *Green Eyes.* The conversation with Pike had suddenly opened a new train of thought—if she could just run down certain vaguely remembered magazine articles. And get the whole thing together in her head. The key word was "telefactor."

Angie taxied north to the Fifties and got out at the branch library across the street from the Museum of Modern Art. The rest of the morning was spent in busy, burrowing research until she joined Jack Bristol at the Çá d' Oro for lunch.

There was much to tell. Jack digested the news of her midnight kidnapping and escape with anxious concern —and the report of her conversation with Laidlaw Pike in frowning puzzlement.

"Am I screwy," he asked over the cannelone, "or does that give Wagner Axby a motive for murder?' "

"How do you mean?"

"If what Pike told you is true, Axby's stage-managing a financial fraud. But it's a cinch Dad would never have gone along with anything like that. He might have blown the gaff—and Axby knew it. So he had Dad killed."

Angie shook her head. "You're forgetting—your father believed the company *was* close to oil. Or so Pike says. According to Pike's story, your father boasted Emerald 'had a strike.' Which would make him Axby's best possible publicity tout and salesman. That's hardly a motive for murder."

"Yeah. You're right. I see what you mean." Jack subsided with a thoughtful scowl—then immediately looked up again at Angie. "Another thing. What about Fergus Doyle? You suppose he's in on this with Axby? . . . Or is Axby conning him, too?"

"I'd like to know the answer to that one myself," mused Angie. "As president and chief executive officer, I suppose Axby might slip one past the chairman and the other directors. On the other hand, it's also possible his only phony move was sending out Pike's expedition —to hot up chances of finding a buyer for the Emerald Oil Company. Maybe your crew actually has found oil."

The Dark Angel smiled—suddenly looking very pretty to her lover and client across the table. "Anyhow, it's all guesswork—and guessing won't get us very far. As of right now, I'm more interested in getting a peek inside Frank Olivet's workshop over in Jersey."

And that was where she and Jack Bristol headed, an hour or so after dark.

Chapter Eighteen

They held hands as the Firebird sped north along the Palisades Parkway.

"I'm still not clear exactly what we're looking for," said Jack.

"Neither am I," Angie admitted. "To tell the truth, I'm just playing a wild hunch. It's so far out I figure it's got to be in."

Near Alpine, they turned off into the Jersey hinterland. Luckily the phone number and address of Olivet's workshop-development lab had been given in the Manhattan phone book along with the listing of his Central Park penthouse. By carefully studying a map they found it without too much difficulty—except for a few hairy moments when they thought they were lost for keeps in the darkness without a compass.

The workshop was set well back from the road among a stand of trees. Its cinder-lane drive was marked only by a slender reflector post and a mailbox bearing the name *Olivet*.

"Looks like he must've picked this place back when he was repairing slot machines for the mob," observed Angie.

The structure consisted of an older wooden half, which looked as if it might once have been a sprawling garage or machine shop, joined at one end to a new cinder-block building. Floodlights on masts cast a pale glow over the property.

"Nothing like working in the full pitiless glare," Angie remarked. The door, in the front of the cinder-block building, was stoutly but not trickily locked. With her nail-file and lipstick burglar tools from her alligator bag, she soon had it open.

Inside they found a wall switch and Jack turned on the light. Apparently this newer building was used largely for office space. It contained a couple of desks with typewriters, an array of business files and an EDP teletype console for a shared-time computer. At the back was a supply room bulging with hardware, metal stock, lumber, electrical parts and a variety of other exotica ranging from a tree surgeon's billhook to a welding company calendar portraying a semi-nude broad fighting off the advances of an apparently amorous police dog bent on disrobing her.

A doorway with a sliding metal fire door connected the two buildings. In the older wooden structure was Olivet's workshop proper. Angie ran her eyes swiftly over its contents. Besides machine tools such as a turret lathe, drill press, power saws and bending brake, there were racks of electronic gear, a laser setup, some ultrasonic equipment, a small forge, a casting tumbler and workbenches hung with hand tools and strewn with work assemblies in various stages of completion. From the forge area near the doorway, curving around into the center aisle of the shop, was an overhead track for an electrically powered chain-fall block. From the block itself hung a long metal housing of some kind, balanced precariously in a cable sling.

The sheer sense of clutter was overwhelming.

"Man, if you're planning to search this layout, we could be here till morning," Jack muttered.

"Too right," agreed Angie. "But at least it won't take a magnifying glass to see what we're after . . . if it's anywhere around."

She led the way down the center aisle, eyes roving from side to side. At the far end of the building was a smorgasbord of junk—old crates, electronic chassis and machine subassemblies stacked next to several trash drums filled with discarded parts.

There was also a large metal shed or cabinet.

"What's in there?" said Jack.

"I wonder."

The shed had a door, but seemingly no handle or latch. Angie got a screwdriver and inserted the blade between the lip of the door and the jamb. There was no give to speak of.

"We could probably break in," she mused, "but it sure as hell wouldn't look the same afterward."

Jack exclaimed, "Hey, what's this?"

"What's what?" Angie half-turned—and her heart gave a small jolt of excitement.

Sonofabitch! They'd struck gold!

Jack was holding a large gray skull, which he had just fished out of one of the trash drums. It looked as if it was molded from fiberglass. He glanced at Angie uncertainly. She twirled her forefinger inside one of its big round eyeholes.

"Ring any bells?" she said.

"My God," said Jack softly. "W–W–Was this the skullhead mask the gunman wore when he shot Dad?"

Angie nodded. "There might be some quibble over your wording, but as a broad general statement—affirmative. Something tells me we'll find what goes with it inside this shed."

"Then, dammit, let's break in."

"Good thinking, baby." She turned back toward the workbenches, seeking a suitable tool to force the door. Her glance fell on a switch panel just above the nearest bench. "Wait a minute," she said to Jack.

"Find something?"

"Maybe we won't have to break in, if one of these does the opening."

The panel was studded with a variety of switches— knobs, toggles, push-buttons. Angie turned one of the knobs. A blast of throbbing rock music flooded the room. Their eyes quickly found the source—quadraphonic speakers, one at each upper corner of the workshop.

Angie grinned and turned down the volume to a pleasantly muted background scoring. "The mobs he worked for were probably into juke boxes and pirating tapes."

She tried another knob—long enough to see the chain-fall block start to move along its tracks. The third turned out to be a master brightness control for the workbench lights. She pushed a button—and a drawer full of drill bits popped out into view from under the workbench. Finally she tried a toggle switch.

The door of the metal shed slid open smoothly.

"Hooray for you," said Jack.

They looked inside. Jack was baffled at the complicated apparatus he saw. Near the door was something that looked like a compact dentist's chair—enclosed within a jointed rig, and topped by a formidable helmet evidently designed to fit over the head of the chair's occupant.

At the back of the shed, beyond the oddball dentist's chair, stood a weird-looking robot.

"What in the bloody hell is all this?" said Jack when he found his voice.

"If I've done my homework correctly, it's a telefactor

robot," said Angie. "The kind we may see walking around on Mars some day."

"I still don't get it."

"Well, let's see if I can explain. To design a robot that can do a lot of difficult tasks on its own is pretty complicated. But engineers can get around that problem by a technique called telefactoring."

"I'm listing. Keep talking."

"With telefactoring," Angie went on, "the robot doesn't have to do things on its own—it's just a *repeater*. The operator straps himself into that chair, with his head inside that helmet thing. The robot's eyes are actually miniaturized TV cameras—which transmit to a television screen inside the helmet, so that the operator sees whatever the robot 'sees.' Then, when he moves his arms or legs or fingers in that jointed rig, radio signals are sent out to the robot—and servo-mechanisms cause it to duplicate whatever movements the operator's making." The Dark Angel grinned at Jack. "Still with me?"

He frowned and scratched his jaw. "Yeah, I think so. Like for instance, the operator watches his TV screen and sees a big rock lying right in the robot's way. So he makes the appropriate movements with his legs, and the robot does likewise—it either steps over the rock or walks around it."

"Right on. That's the general idea," said Angie. "Or, to take an example closer to home—the operator looks at his TV screeen and sees a man sitting inside a house. So the operator moves his hand and forefinger—and the robot points a gun and fires."

"Jesus Christ." Jack looked at Angie. "So that's how it was done."

"It has to be. That skull's no coincidence. It was part of the robot's Halloween disguise."

"What about the bastard who operated the robot?"

"He was down at the foot of the hill—sitting in the back of that van the kids saw."

Frank Olivet?"

"No, Jack," said a man's voice. "It wasn't me who killed your father."

The Dark Angel and Jack Bristol turned with a start. Frank Olivet was standing in the connecting doorway of the workshop with a gun in his hand.

"Sorry you had to find out, kid." With a ghastly rictus that might have been meant for a smile, he added, "I'm afraid Miss Harpe was too smart for your own good."

"Great. You think I'm smart, here's some good advice," said Angie. "If you haven't killed anyone yet, don't start now."

"Don't worry, sweetheart. I have no intention of pulling this trigger—unless one of you makes it necessary. By the way, thanks for turning on the music. That helped me get in here without being heard."

"Don't mention it," said Angie. "The pleasure's all yours. I probably shouldn't ask, but how did you know we were coming?"

"No problem. Have you taken a look at the bottom of your shoulder bag lately?"

"Hell's bells—don't tell me you bugged me?"

"A little stickpin mike-transmitter. My own design, about the size of a nickel." Olivet's face shaped another death's-head smile. "Don't feel too badly, Miss Harpe —I just stuck it on while I was escorting you to the door. You could hardly have noticed."

"Thanks, I'll try to bear up under my chagrin," said Angie. "Mind if I take a look at your masterpiece? I might want to buy some from you if I come out of this alive." She made a tentative move toward her alligator bag sitting on the floor near the workbench.

Olivet's voice whipcracked, "Don't try it, Miss Harpe

—or you won't even live through this little chat we're having. You being a private detective, I would assume you carry a gun in that bag."

"I do, as a matter of fact. A beautiful little Baby Browning. With mother-of-pearl grips. Would you like to see it?"

"I think I could learn to dislike you, Miss Harpe. But fortunately you won't be around long enough for either of us to find out."

Olivet paused. A heavy vehicle could be heard pulling up outside. "Yes, I'm afraid that's them now."

"Whom is them?" said Angie.

"Friends of mine. From earlier days."

"Ah, yes. Your mob connections, I presume."

"Presume what you please, sweetheart. They lent me a man to monitor your bug. He's been on your tail all afternoon. But I imagine this is the cleanup squad."

Two men came into the building. Frank Olivet moved aside from the connecting doorway to let them through into the workshop proper.

"Hiya, Frank baby. Are these our pigeons?" The speaker was a big, unshaven goombah. His partner was harder, younger, more lethal-looking—especially since he was packing a cute little Ingram submachine gun, compared to the other's blued-steel Colt Shooting Master.

"These are the ones," Olivet confirmed. "You two come alone?"

"Nah, Leo's out in the truck keeping his eyes peeled."

"Another of your Jersey lime pit jobs, I presume?" Angie spoke up.

The goombah chuckled good-naturedly. "How 'ja guess, chickie?"

"What's the deal?" said Olivet.

"We got a load of sand out there. Just stick 'em in, that's all. No loud noises, no fuss—they just suffocate

192

nice and quite." The goombah chuckled again. "And when we get there, we open the tailgate and dump. Finito. Capeesh?"

"Congratulations," said Angie. "You rate an E award for efficiency. And A for asshole."

"Okay, go to it," Olivet told the two torpedoes. "I'm going out to talk to Leo. You want to wire their wrists, you'll find some on a reel back there."

"Good enough, Frankie boy. We'll handle it."

Olivet went out.

The two hoods looked at Angie and Jack Bristol. The goombah glanced up at the stereo speakers and chuckled some more. "Even a little musical accompaniment. Should be something more dignified, though—y' know what I mean? Like the Funeral March."

Chapter Nineteen

The broad ain't bad for a jig," said the hood with the Ingram. "It's a shame to waste that kind of pussy."

The goombah grinned. "Who knows? There might be time for a little fun at that, before we take 'em outside."

"You inspire me, boys," said Angie as the two started down the aisle toward her and Jack. "Hold it right there, and let's see if I can't put on a good enough show to change your minds."

They paused appreciatively, giving her time to peel off her sweater.

"I mean if you like pussy, let's talk deal," said Angie. "Who the fuck wants to wind up in a lime pit?"

"You got something there, baby," said the submachine gunner.

"She's got *two* things there," said the goombah, as Angie unhooked her bra and let her big brown breasts pop into view.

Hastily she unzipped her slacks. "Turn the music up, Jack. Maybe a few bumps and grinds will help get things on the right track."

She had their attention now, but Angie knew she had to work fast. For the moment they were willing to stand there and eyeball her, but only as long as she kept them interested.

Jack moved toward the workbench, scowling and torn by conflicting emotions. Goddamn the dirty bastards, watching his lovely Dark Angel undress. On the other hand, he didn't want to wind up in a lime pit any more than she did. And he had a vague, confused feeling that Angie knew what she was up to—and was counting on him to cooperate.

The two mobsters watched him warily out of the corner of their eyes as Jack reached toward the switch panel and turned up the music. They were still far enough down the aisle to be able to bracket both him and Angie within their angle of vision. The stereo speakers were booming now—a mean, throbbing, sweaty Rolling Stones number—perfect for a striptease.

If you could call it a striptease. She hadn't wasted that much time getting down to basics. Her slacks were already off—everything but her colorful little Van Raalte floral-print panties. And she was gradually peeling these down toward the timber line as she jiggled and ground her hips and revolved her rump at her audience.

The two thugs were watching spellbound, greedy-eyed. Which didn't prove they wouldn't spot him if he made a move toward Angie's shoulder bag. To reach it, he'd have to move a step farther along the workbench, then bend slightly from the waist and reach down toward the floor. . . .

"I think we're getting in the groove now, man!" Angie panted out sexily. "Really rollin' down the track!"

The track! Jesus Christ, how could he be so slow on the uptake! Jack's arm barely moved as his fingers twirled the control knob up to full speed.

The chain-fall block jolted into motion. The falls clanked and their load swung precariously as the block came cornering around the curve of the track and into the aisle—but the sound was unnoticeable under the blasting beat of the music. The speakers blared. Angie bumped and ground and shed her pants. The hoods watched, hypnotized. And the chain-fall came zooming down the workshop aisle behind them.

Whammo! The long, heavy machine housing slammed the goombah and his partner in the back, knocking them both face forward to the floor. Jack flicked the control knob off, to slow and halt the juggernaut before it reached Angie.

The younger hood had been hit hardest. He'd landed sprawling on top of his Ingram. But the goombah was already getting up again—dazed but clawing frantically for his Colt .38.

There was no time to go for the Browning in Angie's bag. Jack grabbed a length of ¾-inch steel bar stock from the workbench and hurled it with both hands, like an overweight javelin. It smashed the goombah in the throat and broke his neck.

Angie was lunging up the aisle, stripped to her shoes and ducking below the chain-fall load, to get the Ingram. Its owner was painfully pushing himself upright, still stunned by the whack from behind that had knocked him down. He got his eyes into focus just in time to see Angie's brown hand snatching at the submachine gun. He got his own hand on its metal stock and they struggled viciously for possession.

Angie kicked him in the jaw, but he knew he was fighting for his life now and he had both hands on the gun—one of them on the pistol grip, groping for the trigger. The gun stuttered and kicked in their grasp, coughing out lethal hunks of lead.

Jack shot him in the side with Angie's Browning. The slug blasted in under his arm and tore its way up into his heart, and he flopped to the deck, as dead as his goombah partner.

Angie straightened up, breathless and sweating. "Baby, you're my man!" she grinned at Jack. They met halfway and she fell into his arms and they kissed passionately.

"We can celebrate later," she said after a long moment. "We've still got those two bastards outside to cope with—Olivet and the truck driver."

"You suppose they heard the shots over the music?" asked Jack.

"Dunno. Maybe we can sneak a peek out the window."

There were three windows on each side of the workshop, protected by heavy-gauge wire grilles. They darted to the nearest one and peered out.

"What the hell—!" muttered Angie in disbelief.

They could see the truck clearly in the glow of the floodlights. Its burly driver, in T-shirt and jeans, was hanging halfway out of the cab—head down and looking very defunct. Olivet lay face-up on the ground nearby, also deceased.

"They're dead! Someone's killed them!" gasped Jack, leaping to the obvious conclusion.

Angie looked around just in time to see the fire door slam home across the connecting doorway—and suddenly it also became obvious they were locked in!

She ran down the aisle, followed by Jack. They tugged at the door handle. Too late—it wouldn't move.

"Whoever did it must've jammed the track!" said Angie.

"The same person who killed those two outside! But who the heck is it?" Jack exclaimed.

"We can go into that later. Our big problem right now is to get the hell out of here."

197

"So he can kill us too?"

"Not if we nail him first."

"Let's see if we can spot him."

The Dark Angel grabbed Jack's arm. "No! Stay away from the windows! The sonofabitch may be waiting for us to show."

"So what do we do? Just stand here?"

"No—let's find a way to get this door open."

"How do we know he's not out there in the office—just waiting to gun us down when we do get it open?"

It was an interesting question, and Angie wasn't too sure how to answer it. In any case, she didn't have to because there was a loud crash against the side of the workshop, and the wall buckled inward.

"Good God! What's the nut up to now?" wondered Jack.

The answer to this one came in seconds. A *whooomp*-ing sound of explosive combustion—audible even above the rock music—then flames glaring through the windows on that side.

"Holy Christ!" said Angie. "He rammed the truck into the wall! And now he's fired the gas tank!"

In moments the whole side of the wooden building was ablaze. There was a crash on the other side of the workshop.

"Our Firebird!" gasped Jack.

"Or Olivet's car."

The question was likely to remain academic, because just then came another *boom* of an exploding gasoline tank and flames bit into the facing wall as well. With both sides now engulfed, the old frame building crackled away merrily—the searing heat making Angie and Jack painfully aware they might soon be fried alive in their own fat.

Angie looked around desperately. "Find an ax or

something! Maybe we can batter our way out through the fire door!"

"It's metal!"

"Not solid. It's probably asbestos sandwiched between sheet metal."

Jack seized the first thing that came to mind—the steel bar he had used to kill the goombah. He grabbed it and ran up the aisle and began pounding the end of the bar against the fire door. The door dented and caved in under his battering-ram attack, but showed no imminent sign of puncturing.

"Wait!" yelled Angie. "Maybe this'll do the trick!" She ran to get the Ingram submachine gun and came dashing up the aisle toward him. "Stand back, honey!" She swung the chopper into firing position and held down the trigger while she hemstitched a circle in the door. "Now give it a good hard belt."

Again Jack rammed hard with the steel bar—and went clear through as the circle of metal and asbestos popped out, like an IBM machine holing a punchcard.

"Okay! Out you go, honey!" said Jack.

Angie started to squirm through the hole—then stopped. "My handbag!"

"Go on! I'll get it!" He ran back down the aisle, between the flames which were closing in from both sides of the workshop. He found her bag, snatched it up and got back to the fire door. He had shoved the Browning temporarily into the top of his pants, but now he plucked it out while he stooped to worm his way through the hole.

There was a loud splintering, rending noise behind him and part of the roof fell in, blazing bright yellow and orange. The flames shot up higher and hotter in the draft of ascending hot air from the chimney effect.

Angie helped pull Jack through to the other side, into

the office area. "No sign of our friend, the torch!" she told him.

"Think we can risk going outside?" said Jack.

"We may have to, if it gets much warmer around here. We're targets anyhow, with all this fucking window space."

They ventured out cautiously, guns at the ready, Angie toting the Ingram, Jack clutching the Browning. They stared around into the darkness surrounding the fire- and flood-lit clearing. The only sound now was the roar and crackle of the flames. Waves of heat assailed them from the fiery plasma of the workshop.

Suddenly they heard another sound in the distance—the *vrooom* of an engine, then the thumping, clattering noise of a vehicle being gunned along over rough terrain. They strained to make out the car, but the trees and darkness masked it from view. They heard it reach the highway. With a mournful roar, it sped off into the night.

"There he goes!" said Angie. "The sonofabitch!"

"Clearing out before someone spots the fire and sounds an alarm," said Jack bitterly.

"We'd better do likewise. Thank God we've still got wheels."

The Firebird was standing where they'd parked it. So apparently it was Olivet's car that had been used to ram and ignite the far side of the workshop.

The mob driver, Leo, had been dumped out on his head when his truck was commandeered. He lay a few yards from Olivet. Both had been shot through the head. Angie double-checked for any sign of a pulse, but realized she was wasting her time.

"You think Olivet was telling the truth?" said Jack as they headed toward the Firebird.

"When? What do you mean?"

"When he said he didn't kill Dad."

"Oh, that," said Angie. "Sure, he was telling the truth."

Jack stared at her doubtfully. "How do you know? I mean—how can you be sure?"

"It's obvious. If Olivet wanted to kill someone, why would he bother using a robot?"

"Well . . . to keep from being seen, I suppose."

"His robot was a potential giveaway in itself," Angie pointed out. "In fact it'd probably be easier to trace and identify a robot than a man. So if he used the skull head to disguise *that,* he could just as well have disguised himself the same way." She shook her head. "Nope, there's only one person who'd have any reason to commit murder by telefactoring."

As she broke off to climb into the car, the Dark Angel looked down at herself in sudden dismay. "Jeez, we forgot my clothes in there! I'm motherfuckin' naked!"

Chapter Twenty

The Firebird thrummed along the moonlit wooded high-way. It was 2:07 AM and they were approaching Lake Nippigong.

"It's a bit late to be asking," said Jack, "but what exactly are we going to do?"

"Look for evidence. As things stand now, with Olivet dead and the robot destroyed, we can't prove shit."

"Okay. Spell it out. What do we look for?"

"Well, for openers," said Angie, "the killers would need a van. If there's one at Nippigong, where would they park it?"

Jack thought for a moment. "There's a garage near the house, which you've seen. But they don't keep a van in that—at least not the few times I've had a look inside. Just Fergus's Buick and the Ford Ranchero Nemo uses. It's only a two-car garage."

Angie shrugged in frustration. "They may have gotten rid of the van, of course—that'd be the smart thing to do."

"There *is* another building," Jack mused, frowning. "You can't see it from the house. It's up against the side of that hill at the north end of the lake, where the ground starts getting steep and rocky."

202

"Used for what?"

"I don't know. A storage shed or some such. I think Fergus once said that they keep the winter feed in there —for the birds and deer and other wildlife."

"Worth checking," said Angie. "Can we get to it without being seen?"

"Sure, I think so—if we take that turn-off lane, just before we reach the main gate. It leads up to another little gate near the end of the lake."

"Okay. What can we lose?"

Jack reached over and slipped his hand between Angie's legs. She closed her thighs on it. "Suppose we don't find any van," he murmured. "What're you going to do in this condition?"

"Fuck you maybe. Then go up to the house and ask if I can borrow some clothes from Mrs. Nemo."

Jack couldn't help laughing. "I actually think you're serious. That would sure shake them up!"

"It might. And then you could find some excuse to go out in the garage and check both cars to see if either one's warm. From there on, we'd play it by ear."

Minutes later Jack stopped and opened a gate and turned into a rutted dirt drive. The building he had spoken of loomed ahead, dark and shadowy. They stopped and got out of the Firebird and walked up to the door. It was padlocked.

"Great. And no windows," muttered Jack, shining his car flashlight around. "Or can you jimmy padlocks, too?"

"Find me something sharp, or get my bag. I'll open the fucking thing."

Jack produced a small pocket knife with some "tool" blades and Angie sprang the lock in about two seconds. She unfastened the hasp and Jack dragged the heavy door open.

There was no van inside.

There was something else—very oddly shaped. And so totally unexpected it didn't register with Angie until she noticed the greenish-black irridescent smears and puddles on the bare earth floor.

"For God's sake!" Jack gasped incredulously.

"Is that stuff what I think it is?" said Angie.

"It's oil, all right," Jack stooped to rub a little between his thumb and forefinger.

"And that thing sticking up from the ground?"

"What they cap a well with, to control the flow. It's called a 'Christmas tree.'"

From a sort of brick chimney on the ground rose a cluster of branch-like fittings, studded with valve wheels. From this, a pipe led off toward the rear of the shed.

There was a kerosene lamp on a bench at one side of the shed. Jack lit it so they could see better. The pipe from the Christmas tree was elbowed down and out under the back wall of the shed.

"Where the hell do you suppose it leads?" Angie puzzled.

"Search me. Maybe he's piping it into barrels for the next fuel crisis. Let's see if we can trace it outside."

Jack led the way with his flashlight. From the point where it emerged from the shed, the pipe ran along the ground—almost invisible in the underbrush—and seemed to disappear among a tumble of rocks and boulders on the slope.

Jack scowled and ran his hand through his thick black hair. "For Pete's sake. I don't get it."

"Don't get what?"

"I think I just clued-in to where the pipe goes," said Jack. "But, good Lord, it doesn't make sense!"

"Tell me," said Angie.

She shivered as a night breeze rustled off the lake. Jack slipped an arm around her naked brown body and they started walking back toward the shed.

He said, "I remember Dad mentioning in a letter once that Fergus Doyle's handyman had discovered quite an underground cave system here at the lake—but they'd closed it off for fear some of the bird sanctuary visitors might try exploring it and get hurt."

"A cave system," Angie murmured. "Well, well, well. I thought you said the setup didn't make any sense."

"Why the heck would anyone pump valuable oil down into an underground cave?"

"Foolish question, man. Obviously to keep Emerald Oil from discovering what a valuable property they own —and thereby stop them from crapping up the landscape with drill rigs and bulldozers and Christ knows what all." Angie stopped outside the lighted shed and looked at Jack, whose expression was slightly stunned. "Don't you see, baby? . . . That's why your father was killed. Because someone really did strike oil—not down in Columbia, but right here at Lake Nippigong."

"Quite right, my dear," said Fergus Doyle. "But then I realized the moment I laid eyes on you that you were a highly intelligent young woman—and a dangerous adversary. As well as a very beautiful one."

He had evidently been waiting in the darkness on the far side of the shed. And now he came wheeling around into the soft flickering glow of the kerosene lamp—cradling a 12-gauge Winchester pump gun in his lap. His eyes lingered appreciatively on Angie's lovely breasts and shapely figure.

"For a wheelchair case, you do get around," said the Dark Angel.

Doyle chuckled dryly—almost, it seemed, sadly. "Nemo phoned and reported you two had died at Olivet's workshop. But something told me he was unduly optimistic. His wife Michelle suspected trouble, too. In fact she read bad luck in the bird formations this evening, when the herons flew out of the marsh. She's Indian,

205

you know—half Mohawk, half Seneca. . . . Anyhow, what with one thing and another, there we were, waiting anxiously for Nemo's return. Then I saw the lights of your car going up the side lane—and I knew it was you two."

"So you saddled up your electric wheelchair and came gunning for us," said Angie.

"That's roughly the picture, I'm afraid."

"You admit you killed my father," said Jack with a look of cold hatred.

Doyle made a helpless gesture. "I don't expect you to understand, my boy. It was the hardest decision of my life. Your father, Lang Bristol, was my friend—my old and valued friend. He meant a great deal to me. You know that. But all this means a great deal to me, too" —he waved vaguely toward the lake—"this bird and animal sanctuary I've worked so hard to develop. At least Lang had *you* to show for his time on earth. With Rose gone, our boy gone, I had nothing left. My life has been an exercise in futility. Even our company, Emerald Oil, has gone steadily downhill in recent years. But if I can preserve this sanctuary, then at least I've done my bit for nature and the ecology—and I can leave something of value to future generations."

"Spare me your self-serving, dime-store philosophy," said Jack.

"I'm only trying to explain. So far, you see, the company's been content to let me stay here, free of charge. Originally this property was bought in a package deal, in connection with some western New York oil leases. It was never seriously considered for development. It made a useful tax writeoff, and the wildlife sanctuary was a nice PR gimmick. But for myself, I wanted something more stable and lasting. I'm dying of bone cancer—perhaps you didn't know that. So I wanted the firm knowledge that I could live out my two or three remaining years of life here—with the land deeded over for an eventual park and public monument, under the name of the Fergus J. Doyle Bird & Wildlife Sanctuary. It seemed a fair retirement gesture after my years of service to the Emerald Oil Company."

"Wouldn't Axby go along?" asked Angie.

Doyle shrugged. "I suppose one can't blame him. Our wells were running dry, the company was in bad straits. And Axby's no man to give away a red cent out of mere sentiment."

"What was wrong with you *buying* the property?" said Jack harshly. "Did you ever consider that?"

"Often, but how could I? My personal fortune, or what's left of it, is tied up in company stock. The directors wouldn't accept that in payment—they knew only too well its value was far lower than the public realized. Nor could I dump it on the market and sell without precipitating a company disaster."

"And that, I presume," said Angie, "is how things stood when Lang Bristol found oil on the property."

Doyle gave a nod. "You've guessed it, my dear. One day last fall he was strolling on marshy ground over there, and suddenly found oil on his shoes. The stuff was literally bubbling out. If you ever knew Lang, you could imagine how that excited him—stumbling on an oil strike, right in Emerald's own backyard."

"And there you sat, peeing in your pants," said Angie inelegantly. "What did you do?"

"It was a bad moment, I assure you. At one terrible blow, I saw my last hopes for the Wildlife Sanctuary go glimmering. But finally I persuaded Lang to wait and say nothing, so I could spring the strike as a surprise at our next board meeting—which wasn't to be until the following month."

"And meantime," gritted Jack Bristol, "you arranged to kill him."

"Yes, there wouldn't be much point in denying it now," said Doyle. "Being a wheelchair cripple, of course, posed quite a problem. Then I remembered the telefactoring experiments that Frank Olivet had carried out for NASA—including a feasibility study which involved construction of an actual test robot."

"So you decided to cash in some long-standing IOUs."

"If you mean by that, I turned to Olivet for help—yes. He owed his career to me, really. And now I was asking him to help save the most important thing left in my life. . . . Mind you, I didn't say *why* I wanted to use the robot, or give him any details. And Frank asked no questions. But he must have known from the urgency and secrecy of my request that it had to be a killing. And when he heard the news of Lang Bristol's murder, I'm sure he knew immediately who'd done it."

"All of which, I gather, didn't faze him?" said Angie.

"Oh, Frank didn't like being a party to Lang's murder—I'm sure it troubled him. But it wasn't all that much of a moral crisis, either. After all, as a young man, he'd been a mob employee—and no doubt this wasn't his first experience of a rub-out. And I'll say this for Frank, when he makes up his mind to help a friend, he doesn't quibble or stint. He even had his gang friends get me a van with false plates—and dispose of it afterward."

"Nemo drove, I suppose, while you sat in back?"

"That's right—I was strapped in with the control apparatus and the robot. Once Frank showed me how to work the telefactor, there was no problem. We parked near the foot of the hill at Lang's summer place. The robot went out the back of the van and returned as soon as the job was done."

"Did you know Dad would offer such a perfect target there at his TV set?" Jack put in.

"No, the window shot was pure chance. My original plan was to have the robot ring the bell, and when Lang answered the door, to shoot him at point blank range."

"Anyhow," said Angie, "once you'd killed him, you thought you had your problem all solved and your secret was safe. But then the rumors started about an Emerald Oil strike."

"Exactly," said Doyle. "Evidently Lang had talked in his cups—no doubt dropping little hints and enjoying people's mystification. Naturally everyone jumped to the conclusion we'd made a strike in Colombia, where we'd carried out our last prospect."

"A nuisance for you maybe," said Angie, "but those rumors also created a great little opportunity to puff your company stock. We already know, by the way, about Axby financing Pike's expedition."

For the first time, Fergus Doyle had the grace to look ashamed. "Maybe you can see now, my dear," he said, "why it caused me no pain to watch you make a fool of Wagner Axby. The man's a contemptible crook. That became only too clear—painfully clear—when he proposed his bargain to me."

"What sort of bargain?"

"That we not only finance Pike's prospect but send out a second expedition of our own. You see his game, of course. He proposed to capitalize on all those wild rumors, so as to create a deliberate fradulent impression that we were onto a major new oil strike in Colombia. And, to heighten that impression, he proposed we apply to Fox Wineburg for a new stock issue—as if we wanted money to start leasing and drilling."

"You spoke of a bargain?" Angie prodded.

"Quite so. Axby forced me to go along with all this if I ever hoped to make the Fergus J. Doyle Wildlife Sanctuary a reality. In return, once we'd attracted a buyer for the company—then and only then—he promised to have the board of directors deed the Lake Nippigong property over to me as a retirement gift."

"A temptation I'm sure you found it hard to resist."

The old man's face hardened. "It may be difficult for you to realize, Miss Harpe, how much this sanctuary means to me. But at any cost I intend to keep it as a preserve for nature's creatures."

"The Fergus J. Doyle preserve for nature's creatures. Don't forget the most important part of it, daddy. But I can see you haven't—otherwise you wouldn't be toting that shotgun."

"I'm prepared to use it too, my dear—make no mistake about that. For the moment my intention is to wait until Nemo returns and let him deal with you. Evidently you passed him on your way here—perhaps while he was phoning me. But if you attempt to escape or make any suspicious moves—believe me, you'll get this full charge of buckshot—at murderous range."

The flicker of Angie's and Jack's eyes must have given away her approach. Doyle jerked his head slightly as if aware that someone was coming up behind him. But his face still showed shock as a woman's voice said:

"No, Fergus. You'll shoot no one—because I have the other shotgun aimed right at the back of your head. There'll be no more killing till I know exactly what's happened—and I mean *everything* that's happened. I want the whole story—from Nemo's own mouth."

Nemo's wife Michele stepped into the glow of light from the shed. She was wearing jeans and an old flannel shirt, with her black hair plaited into two Indian braids. She had a Remington poised for a fast blast, like a hunter about to flush a pheasant—and she looked as if she'd learned to use it expertly in pre-sanctuary days.

"Of course you want the whole story. Michele," Doyle said smoothingly. "you're involved in this as much as Nemo or myself—and you have as much at stake. Surely you realize we can't leave these two alive."

"Don't worry, I'll keep them covered till Nemo gets here," she retorted. "And you too, old man. Now slide that gun away from you. . . . Carefully, so there'll be no accidents."

Doyle tried to argue, but the Indian woman's voice was firm. Finally he obeyed, sullenly and with a show of indignation. "My God, Michele, don't you trust me—after all I've done for Nemo?"

"Nemo repaid you in full when he helped you kill this boy's father."

"He was helping himself too!" Doyle fumed. "And *you*, for heaven's sake! You know you'll inherit everything I leave. I promise you—it's written into the terms of the codicil that you'll be official caretakers of this place as long as you live."

"That's what I'm afraid of—you and your goddamned promises!" Michele flared back viciously. "Nemo was a good man once. A kind decent human being—in spite of all he's suffered. Until you corrupted him. And now you've turned him into a lousy, stinking mass murderer!"

"Damn it, you're talking nonsense! He went down to Olivet's lab to help make sure these two were silenced, that's all. As you see, they apparently escaped. So now they'll have to be dealt with here. What else can we do?"

"He's leaving out a few small details," Angela Harpe broke in. "Nemo didn't just drop down to make sure Jack and I got wasted. Maybe that's the jive they handed you, Mama, but it sure as hell isn't what happened. There are four corpses down there in Jersey—Olivet and three mob soldiers that he called in to dispose of us."

"All of whom you doubtless killed while escaping!" Doyle tried to beat down her words with his own.

"The fuck we did," Angie snapped back. "Jack and I were inside the workshop trying to cope with two of them. Olivet and the driver were outside. Michele's old man shot them both in cold blood. Then he locked the workshop and tried to incinerate the rest of us—just to make sure there'd be no one left—not even your dear old friend Olivet, who might tattletale inconveniently."

Michele's eyes were wide with horror.

"She's lying!" Doyle's voice had gone shrill. "Her story's absurd. You know your husband's not capable of such barbarous behavior, Michele. Nor have I 'corrupted' him, as you so quaintly put it."

"I hope you haven't, Fergus," Michele said in a soft but deadly voice. "Because if you have—*you're* the one who's in the most danger."

"What the devil does that mean? What are you talking about?"

"That nightcap I gave you to drink tonight while we were waiting for Nemo, remember? Did you know he mixed it for you himself before he left this evening? . . . I couldn't help wondering why, because normally he always lets me prepare it for you when he's out. But not this time. And he told me—'*The medicine's already in it.*'"

Now it was Fergus Doyle whose eyes showed horror But he stubbornly resisted Michele's insinuation. "What's so strange about that? Nemo has standing orders to put in four drops of my prescription medicine each night."

Michele smiled grimly. "I know, old man. But this is the *first* time since Axby signed over the deed awarding you this property—including the oil well he doesn't even know about. And you haven't voided your old will yet, naming Nemo and me as your sole heirs."

She paused and moved around closer into the light so

she could observe the effect on Doyle better, while still keeping Angie and Jack covered with her shotgun.

"Are you thinking the same thing I am, Fergus? That maybe this time it wasn't your *regular* medicine Nemo put in your nightcap? . . . Maybe he put in that other stuff your doctor slipped you, off the record—the potassium chloride in case the pain gets too bad for you to bear."

Doyle's lips moved slowly without any words coming out, as if he couldn't quite get himself together. "Wh–Wh–What the devil are you suggesting?"

It was a question Michele didn't really need to answer. And she got no chance to, anyway—because just then Nemo came hulking up out of the darkness.

Chapter Twenty-One

With his enormous size and misshapen head, Nemo looked like something out of a comic-book nightmare. Angie saw that he was holding a .22 Ruger. Probably the gun that killed Jack's father. Not to mention Olivet and Leo.

Fergus Doyle's face had gone gray. "My God, is this true, Nemo?" he gasped. "That you put potassium chloride in my drink tonight?"

The giant grunted, "Eff. Hit hroo."

Doyle suddenly maneuvered his wheelchair toward the shotgun he'd discarded at Michele's command.

"Stop him, Nemo!" she shouted. "We don't want to shoot him!"

Angie tugged Jack's sleeve and signaled with her eyes. They turned and bolted into the darkness.

Behind them, from the shed, came the sounds of a scuffle, a grunted curse—then the single blast of a shotgun.

By this time, Angie and Jack were clambering up the hillside among the trees and rocks and underbrush. Branches slapped and tore at Angie's naked flesh. She ignored the pain. Who gave a damn about sharp branches? Better a few scratches than an ass full of buckshot!

They paused, panting, in the darkness, unable to see what was going on below. At least Doyle's diversion had given them precious moments to put space between themselves and their captors. But they both knew with terrifying certainty that Monster Man would soon be after them.

Dammit, if only they could get their hands on that Ingram submachine gun in the Firebird! Or even Angie's Baby Browning! But there was no chance as long as anyone stayed posted by the shed.

"Look!" Jack whispered as he caught his breath. "How about you getting up there?" He pointed to a jagged rocky outcrop on their right, projecting baldly out from the face of the hillside in a series of slabs and shelves and craggy upthrusts.

"Why? What's the advantage?" Angie whispered back.

"He's not apt to look up there. Ten to one he'll just take it for granted we'll cling to cover. When we hear him coming, I'll make some noise among the trees and brush and try to lead him off in the opposite direction. Maybe one or the other of us can get back to the car and grab a gun."

Angie hesitated, worried and uncertain. What Jack was proposing made sense in a way. But there was also safety in numbers—especially against an opponent like Nemo. Still, his strategy might double their chances of getting a gun . . . which in the long run was damn near a necessity if they hoped to get out of this fucking mess alive.

"Come on! Do it!" Jack urged.

"Okay, baby! Just be careful!"

He hoisted her up and gave her a parting kiss on the left cheek as she clambered to the rock platform above.

Just in the nick of time! Someone was coming up the slope directly below them. Jack melted off into the darkness among the shadowy trees and shrubbery. Angie threw herself flat on the slatey rock.

It was Nemo, all right! She could hear him thudding up the slope, pushing shrubbery aside, cracking twigs underfoot. In a few moments he was nearing the spot where she and Jack had just paused for their whispered conference.

Nemo was pausing, too. Listening. She could damn near spit on the jive turkey from where she was lying.

From somewhere off in the distance came a rustle of brush—Jack's ploy to draw the giant away.

Angie could almost tangibly sense Nemo's response —the barely audible hiss of breath, the sudden tensing of muscles. The atmosphere changed, too—as if a jolt of electricity had arced through the air, the moment hunter made contact with hunted.

And then Angie's right foot jerked, as a cramp spasm twitched the calf muscle of her leg. A fine spatter of gravel and grit went trickling across the slate and down off the rock shelf.

She froze. But Nemo had heard it. To hell with that noise in the brush—he wanted to know what was lurking just above him. He put the shotgun up first, then grabbed the edge of the rock itself and swung himself up into view.

Holy jumping Jesus! What a horror-movie gorilla! His sudden ascent had taken Angie by surprise. She lay there half-paralyzed with indecision. . . . What the fuck was she supposed to do now? Play dead?

She was lying on one side in dense shadow, with her back up against the next rise of rock. But Monster Man had seen her, all right. And then like a gift from God, Angie's hand closed on a hunk of stone the size of a baseball.

Aiiyeeeee! With a tigerish scream, she hurled the rock straight at Nemo. It hit him in the face—and he stumbled a step backward, heeling into the shotgun, sending it clattering into the brush below. Angie leaped up with another yell, kicked him hard in the gut and almost in the same sweep of motion scrambled up to the next rock ledge above.

Christ, she hadn't even taken the wind out of him! The bastard was coming right after her! And he was no clumsy slob, either—he moved his huge bulk with speed and precision, like a fucking two-ton mountain goat!

What to do? There was sure as hell no room up here for graceful aikido twirls and springboard karate leaps —not in the cramped darkness on these uneven platforms and ledges.

Angie glanced around frantically for a makeshift weapon as she clambered upward, keeping a few yards above and ahead of her giant pursuer.

What was that, sticking out up there? . . . Hey, right on! Some kind of thick, weathered piece of tree branch that had rolled down from the woods farther up the hillside.

Angie grabbed it and whirled around just as Nemo came grunting and clawing his way after her. She jabbed the stick at him like a spear without even stopping to think—and laid open his cheek from ear to mouth. Before he could snatch it from her, she yanked the branch back again.

Next time, she swung it like a baseball bat, belting him across his cockeyed skull. The thud sounded like a sure shot to the bleachers.

Nemo bellowed with pain and rage. He grabbed the branch away from her and hurled it down the slope. Angie hauled ass for higher ground.

Oh, God! End of the line! Straight ahead was a rock rise too high to get up without some real acrobatics— and there was no time for that. Or she could go for a high dive off Lover's Leap if she preferred. Sheeee-*yit!*

Angie glanced back. Nemo was coming on fast. Her eyes probed desperately. There were some jagged rock handholds jutting out up there—but she'd have to play this by ear now. Monster Man was right up her tailpipe.

All right, if that's how it had to be. She whirled to face him and steeled her thoughts. *You hammer-headed sonofabitch! You're gonna hurt from your ass to your eyeballs before you ice me!*

A banshee shriek ripped from her lungs as she charged him—one hand out stiff for a *nukite* sword thrust. Nemo stopped short in sheer amazement. The sword thrust went deep into his solar plexus, and the giant doubled, gasping for breath. Angie chopped him across the neck and brought her clenched fists down on the back on his skull. Incredibly the bastard just shook it off, like a spaniel shaking water!

His tree-trunk arms went around her. His face was greasy with blood from his ripped cheek, and her stone throw must have broken his nose. Oh, Jesus! Her ribs were cracking! Her knee rammed home to his nuts, and once again she heard him bellow in agony. Still his grip held. She could no longer breathe. He was lifting her up for a throw. Angie bit him in the throat—no fancy fucking vampirish love bite, but an animal clamp on his juglar, like a feral wolf, lips drawn back from its fangs, going in for the kill.

Nemo let out a ghastly hoarse shriek from his ravaged vocal cords. He let go of his bear hug and grabbed Angie by the hair, trying to rip her away from his throat. Her fingers clawed into his eyes, and he hurled her away.

She danced backward, orienting herself by instinct and sixth sense to those rocky handholds she'd noticed. Nemo came lunging at her like a charging bull. Angie leaped aside, grabbed the handholds and swung her legs in a vicious roundhouse kick that caught him at the back of his skull as he roared past her. No chance to step on the brakes—he couldn't stop. His intended target was no longer there to resist him as expected, and her kick had jolted him off-balance, adding to his forward momentum. With a yell of terror, he went over the edge!

Angie heard his dying shriek as he bounced off the rocks, from ledge to ledge, then went smashing on down through the brush and trees to a full stop somewhere at the foot of the hillside.

She dropped from her handholds and stood there sucking air into her tortured lungs. Then her head drooped and her shoulders slumped. She let herself go limp all over, emptying herself of will, emptying her mind of all thoughts, save the great all-encompassing One.

A moment passed, extending itself toward infinity like a sustained resonant chord. . . .

Then she was herself again, opening her eyes and straightening her shoulders—back once more in the night world of Lake Nippigong, but refreshed and cleansed by her brief contact with the Source.

She knew by some deep instinct now that there was no longer anything to fear. She made her way leisurely, without effort, down off the rock face and back to the wooded greenery of the hillside.

"*Ja-a-a-ack!*" she called, cupping her hands. Her words echoed through the darkness from the trees and rocks. "*I'm going back to the shed!*"

At the bottom of the hill, Michele was kneeling over Nemo's battered corpse. She glanced around. Angie saw in the dappled moonlight that she was holding the Ruger .22.

For one heart-stopping moment the Dark Angel wondered if her intuition had fatally misled her. But Michele straightened to her feet and made no move to use the piece.

"Don't worry," she said wearily. "The killing's over." She let the gun drop from her hand.

"What about Fergus Doyle?" said Angie.

"Dead. From the potassium chloride Nemo put in his drink."

Jack came walking out of the darkness to join them.

"Let me see if I have this straight," said Angie. "Your husband poisoned Doyle?"

The Indian woman nodded. "But the police need never know. Unless you tell them. His doctor will write up the death certificate as due to natural causes. He was the one who gave Fergus the stuff—to take when the pain got out of hand. And the timing will make it seem all the more natural."

"What do you mean, the timing?" Jack asked her.

"Staroleum's buying out the Emerald Oil Company," Michele explained, "so today Axby deeded over this property to Fergus Doyle. It'll look as if the old man was hanging on just long enough to make his wildlife sanctuary a permanent reality."

"Originally," said Angie, "Doyle made a will naming Nemo and you as his sole heirs. Is that right?"

"Yes—but once he got the deed from Axby, he had a codicil ready, leaving this property to the government. Of course, if he died before the codicil was executed, then Nemo and I stood to inherit this property—and the oil well."

"And *has* the codicil been executed?"

"It's written and signed in Doyle's own hand and witnessed by us—but it hasn't yet been mailed to his lawyer. Nemo, of course, would have destroyed it."

"And now Nemo's dead too," said Angie. "I wonder if they'll rule his death accidental?"

"Why not? He was up there climbing among the rocks, trying to forget his grief over the death of his

master and dear old friend. Either he lost his balance—
or his mental stability."

"Which leaves you sole heir," mused Angie. "Will
you destroy the codicil?"

"It's up at the house—in a stamped envelope on the
fireplace mantel. Take it with you and drop it in the
mailbox if you like." Michele turned away. "And now
please get the hell out of here."

She sank to her knees and began crooning a slow, ee-
rie Indian death chant over Nemo's body.

Fergus Doyle sat peaceful and relaxed and dead in his
electric wheelchair, head drooping on his chest, waiting
to be wheeled back to the gray fieldstone house overlooking Lake Nippigong.

Jack Bristol and the Dark Angel got into the Firebird
and drove slowly away.

"Should we stop by the house for that codicil?" said
Jack.

"Hell, no," said Angie. "If the government gets this
property, some horse's ass will discover that oil well. If
Michele inherits, I think it'll stay a wildlife sanctuary.
Let's leave it to the birds."

Self help & reference

Excitement Reading